ANOTHER LAST DAY

Don Levin

authorHOUSE®

AuthorHouse™
1663 Liberty Drive
Bloomington, IN 47403
www.authorhouse.com
Phone: 1 (800) 839-8640

Published by AuthorHouse 11/07/2016

ISBN: 978-1-5246-4776-6 (sc)
ISBN: 978-1-5246-4774-2 (hc)
ISBN: 978-1-5246-4775-9 (e)

Library of Congress Control Number: 2016917988

Print information available on the last page.

All scriptures are taken from King James Version of the bible.

0600

"Sing like no one's listening,
Love like you've never been hurt,
Dance like nobody's watching,
And live like its Heaven on Earth."

—Mark Twain

You are going to die today.
What?
You are going to die today.
That's crazy. Nobody gets told ahead of time when they are going
to die.
Sometimes when it is deemed warranted, advance notice is given.
Who decides that?
A power greater than both of us.

The sting of the water in the shower felt good on his tired muscles. The shower 'room' and spa in the master suite of his home had long since been a final refuge for Jack going back to the days when he was still practicing law, and the stress associated with his job had nearly destroyed his marriage and prompted weekly visits to chiropractors, massage therapists, and at one point a cardiologist. The shower had been a refuge against the phone, the e-mail, and sometimes even the family. It provided the final refuge that he could not even find on the golf course because nobody would dare come talk to him while he was in the shower.

The steam billowed up to the ten foot ceiling, swirling and forming clouds around the humidity protected light, as drops of mist fell back toward his upturned face. The workout he had just completed had been one of the harder ones of late, but he felt good. Business was good, his stress levels minimal, and aside from the familiar twinge in his right knee, all was right with the world.

He had experienced that occasional sharp pang in the heart again this morning, but it was *before* he had mounted the elliptical, and it had quickly passed. More annoying than anything else, it nonetheless always got his attention.

"An irregular heart valve sequence" is what the doctor had called it twenty five years ago when Kathy had rushed him to the ER after calling her mother to come and watch the two kids. The tests at the hospital had been inconclusive and he had felt redeemed because he knew that it was nothing. The doctor went on to confirm these results the next day in his private office, and said that Jack would have it for the rest of his life and when he got to be 'older' that he might confuse it for a real heart attack that could very well kill him. No treatment, no corrective surgery, no meds, just something that he would have to learn to *live* with, much like some people learn to live with a trick knee or elbow.

Now a fully *recovered* attorney, he was completely comfortable in his new career, selling houses. A couple three sales a year in the high end market and it was far less stress, a lot easier money, and allowed for a whole lot more time to play golf, fool around with their very modest speedboat, and to see more of the kids and grandkids.

Not to mention which, nobody makes realtor jokes. He still remembered all of the punchlines to the myriad of attorney jokes that he had had to endure over the years:

"What do you call one thousand attorneys up to their necks in sand on the beach?" A: Not enough sand.

"What do you call one thousand attorneys on the bottom of the ocean?" A: a good start.

"Why can lawyers swim unharmed in shark-infested waters?" A: professional courtesy.

One of his friends had thought to send him at least one attorney joke every day for nearly ten years. At one point he had seriously considered forming a compilation of this ridiculous humor and marketing it, but had abandoned the idea when he realized that he personally resented the humor that came at the expense of a lot of *good* and *honest* attorneys who had to suffer the sling and arrows that should have been directed at only a small number of those who labored under the guise of counselors at law.

Jackson Davis Lee. His parents, born and bred in Richmond VA, like their parents before them, had never quite given up on the fact that the "War of Northern Aggression," or that "recent unpleasantness" had ended with the South at the losing end of the score. All four boys in his family bore the names of Confederate generals. As the oldest, he was lucky. He was named for Thomas "Stonewall" Jackson and President Jefferson Davis, two men clearly dedicated to their duty.

After obtaining an Army commission through ROTC at Virginia Commonwealth University, and during a stint in the Army, Jack had married Kathy, his high school sweetheart, and they had started their life and family together while he attended law school in Charlottesville, VA at the University of Virginia Law School. Twenty years of practice had been hard on him, as well as the family, and had nearly fractured his marriage on a couple of occasions when protracted trials had kept him away from them for long periods of time.

At age 51, after burying yet another friend who had died of a premature heart attack, Jack had taken down the shingle, and had transitioned to a career in high-end residential real estate.

Today at age 57, he had been told by a voice only present in his head that he was going to die.

0640

"We may be surprised at the people we find in heaven. God has a soft spot for sinners. His standards are quite low."

—Desmond Tutu

Am I really going to die today?

Yes Jack. Knowing this is a great gift.

Gift? Dying is a gift? Knowing ahead of time is a gift? That's crazy.

Some would beg to differ with you. Some would literally sacrifice everything for literally only a minute's warning.

Okay, so when am I going to die?

Today.

But when today am I going to die?

Today.

Can you give me a time?

Would it matter?

Well yeah. It would be nice to know how much time I have left.

You just said that knowing is not a gift. Isn't it enough to know that sometime today you are going to die and that you have only a finite amount of time in which to act?

Exactly my point. How much time do I have?

More than you think...

What does that mean?

Nobody ever plans on dying. They often leave unfinished business. You my friend have been given a great gift in that you can leave this earth with no unfinished business.

Unfinished business?

You know, regrets, things unsaid, things left undone.

I don't think I have any regrets.

Sure you do Jack. Everyone has regrets. Let's face it, everyone is busy. Life gets away from us. There is always something that keeps us from getting to something else important. How many times did you have to choose between work and family? How many times did you have to choose between 'good, better, best?'

Sometimes we have to sacrifice the short term for the long term.

My point exactly Jack. There is always something to distract us from getting around to doing something else that needed doing at the same time. A lot of people would simply call that Life.

I think we made pretty good choices when it came to our family and did a good job of juggling sports, and school, and work, and the house, and chores, and the million other things that suck up our time.

I don't disagree Jack, but let's face it, there were times when you missed this, that, or the other thing because you were in trial, or away for the Army, or running late to the soccer game, and missed the birthday party.

I did my best. They understood.

No doubt Jack. But this is what we mean by regrets. Look at you now; two cell phones and a blackberry. Between Facebook, LinkedIn, Twitter, and e-mail, you are even more distracted.

These are tools that I use for work. Real Estate is like that; nobody looks at houses in a book anymore. It's all electronic, and timing is everything.

I know Jack. But remember when Greg had his heart attack, and you visited with him in the hospital? You were pretty shaken up. After all, he was only 43.

And recovered because he was in good shape.

Yes, but it scared you.

Heck yeah it did. I mean we used to play racquetball together. He was a bull.

And now?

We play a more sedate game, but we still play.

But how did you feel when you left the hospital that day?

I was upset at seeing a good friend struck down in his prime.

And what did you promise Kathy?

That I would take better care of myself, and that I would not go down like Greg had gone down.

But how did you feel?

What do you mean 'feel?'

You know what I mean. What emotions or regrets did you experience?

Well, uh, I naturally felt bad for some of the things that I had done, or not done, or had hoped to do.

Those are called regrets. I think we need to discuss this point more fully.

I really don't think I have too many regrets.

Really? I don't meet too many people who don't have at least a few regrets from their life.

Well, no more than anyone else I suspect.

What comes to mind right now?

Well, if I am really going to die today, I guess I would have to say not taking better care of my health when I had the chance would have to be a regret. But I work out, watch what I eat, don't drink, well too much, never did drugs, and only smoke an occasional cigar. Never smoked cigarettes or grass. I would imagine that you probably hear this one a lot.

Nobody ever inhales…

I mean years ago, when I thought I was having a heart attack and it turned out to be nothing, I made a promise to myself and to Kathy that I would do an even better job taking care of myself, and I did. Are you sure I am going to die today?

Quite sure.

It sure doesn't seem fair. After all, I have tried to do right by myself in terms of exercise and diet, and now you are telling me that it didn't matter.

It all matters.

Sure doesn't seem right.

Any other regrets come immediately to mind?

I remember when I was in fifth grade and was getting bullied at school by Charles O'Shea.

Oh yes, Charles O'Shea.

Never Charlie, never Chuck. But Charles. He was a mean bugger. He terrorized most of the class. He was so much bigger than the rest of us. I remember dreaming about beating the tar out of him in front of the entire class, just to teach him a lesson.

To teach him a lesson, or to humiliate him as he had humiliated you?

Probably both. I just remember running home from school afraid of getting caught by the guy. It was a horrible way to live.

What happened?

My dad told me to stand up for myself, and to not be afraid.

How did that work out?

You know how it worked out. He chased me until I fell and tore the knee out of my pants and then picked me up and punched me until my nose was bleeding and I was crying. The worst of it was that my dad was disappointed that I didn't get enough licks of my own in, and of course my mother freaked out and slapped me for tearing my pants. It was a banner day all the way around. Thanks for making me remember it.

If it makes you feel any better, Charles died twenty years ago.

Oh really? How?

In a bar fight. Apparently he was making unwanted advances towards a young lady, and her date that night was defending her honor. Charles pulled out a knife, and the date pulled out a gun. Seems he was an off-duty sheriff's deputy who didn't take kindly to being threatened with deadly force. Shot Charles square in the chest, and when Charles didn't go down and in fact seemed to get angrier and more intent on stabbing the deputy, he shot him a second time. He died in the bar.

Hmm. Sounds like he got what was coming to him.

Some might say that. Live by the sword, die by the sword, and all that, but he was still someone's son, and brother, and a child of God.

Black sheep maybe. And dumb.

Dumb?

The dumbest thing to bring to a gunfight is a knife, he said with a smirk.

Any other regrets?

One. I've carried it with me for forty years now.

Mike?

Yeah, how did you know? Oh, yeah, dumb question.

Tell me about it anyway.

Not a lot to tell. When I was in high school there were four of us who hung out. We were fairly inseparable. David and Louis who were brothers, and of course Mike. Mike had moved out of the city to live with his grandparents because some of the gangs in the city had taken a distinctive dislike to him. They make Charles O'Shea look like a pussy cat. Well, I graduated high school after three years because I had the credits and I was bored. I started college in the city, and between working full-time and part-time and keeping up with ROTC and oh yeah, an occasional bit of studying, I sort of lost touch with them. I mean I would see them once in a great while, but they were still in high school, and I was in college, and well, you know, we sort of moved in different circles.

Mike loved you guys as if you were his own brothers. He was an only child.

I know. Well, I was actually home during Spring Exams week, and when I was not studying, I was working crazy hours trying to stash extra cash. It was Tuesday, April 20th, and it was lunchtime. I was at the house with my girlfriend.

Kathy?

No. Kathy was dating someone else at this point in time. We had sort of decided to take a timeout, and let's just say that she didn't sit at home pining away for me. I was with Debbie that day.

And?

Well, this girl was someone I worked with, and was a bit of a wild child, and we both started at 1:30 that day, so she was all for us going to this hot dog joint that we all liked a lot, and having a dog and a brew before work.

And...

I had this really strong feeling that we should go see Mike, but when I suggested it, she said that she was hungry and that we really didn't have time to see him and have lunch.

So you went for lunch.

Yeah. And then went to work, but had this nagging feeling that I had messed up somehow. I was a stock clerk and Tuesday was a big order day for us so I got busy and before I knew it, it was time for my dinner break.

What happened?

Well, I grabbed a sandwich out of the vending machine, studied for twenty minutes, and went back to work. I was on the floor stocking the order that had come in, when I was paged to pick up the store phone. And...

And what?

And I knew it was not going to be good. It was against company policy to take personal calls, and I had told my family to never call me at work and so when the page was for me and not for my department, I knew it was trouble.

Who was it?

Lisa. Another girl I had dated. She was a junior, so a year behind our group in school.

Go on.

I could tell that she had been crying. She was a sweet girl with a big heart. She then said, 'I thought you should know that Mike is dead.' My heart nearly stopped. I went completely numb. My throat closed up. All I could do was croak out the single word 'how?'

Did she know?

Oh yeah. She knew. Seems that my good friend Mike had had enough of the ridicule of the "beautiful people" in our new school, and was feeling more than a little alone, and finally decided that he wasn't going to deal with it any longer.

What did he do?

YOU know what he did. He sat in his 1928 Model A in the garage of his grandparent's house with the door closed, and gave himself the big sleep.

'I thought you should know. I thought you should know. I thought you should know.' Those words haunted me for years.

Why?

Guilt. Guilt, guilt, guilt.

What happened next?

Well, I finished my shift, clocked out a little before 10:00 that night, and couldn't say a word to anyone. I didn't trust myself to say or do anything except to face the shelves. I was like a zombie.

What did you do then?

I drove home like a madman at like 70 miles an hour. Debbie called home, and even though she was nineteen, her parents still kept her under their thumb. She got permission to keep me company, and she followed me in her car.

What did you do?

Oh, I basically cried or rambled on about Mike for about four hours. The ultimate soliloquy complete with ranting about how I – I never said she or we – was responsible for his death.

Why did you feel responsible?

Because Lisa told me that they had already calculated that he did it on his lunch hour from school – about noon time – *exactly* when I was prompted to go over and see him.

You didn't know…

Yes I did. Had I gone over there, I could have stopped him.

Only until the next time he was feeling despondent.

And maybe I would have been prompted again to save him.

Maybe so, but probably not. You were not Mike's keeper.

If nothing else, he wouldn't have done what he did on my watch that day.

Any other regrets regarding Mike?

Actually, no.

Why not?

Well, the next day I went to the funeral home and I remember this like it was yesterday mind you. I walked in and there was Mike's dad standing at the casket, stroking Mike's face, all the while the very *beautiful people* who had ridiculed Mike were there, prancing around as if they were his best friends, and that this was a social event at which they needed to be seen.

What did you do?

I was enraged. I very quietly told Mike's dad that these people, whom he thought were Mike's friends, did not belong there, and that I was going to have them asked to leave or be physically removed if necessary, or throw them out myself.

And they left?

With enough drama to win themselves an Oscar. No regrets there.

Did you attend the funeral?

Couldn't.

Why not?

I had an exam scheduled for that day.

Couldn't you reschedule it?

Oh yeah. I even talked to the professor who was very understanding and said to merely send his secretary a copy of the obituary and that I could take a makeup exam at the beginning of the next semester. He wasn't even going to make me wait to take it like some Profs do at the end of the next semester.

So why didn't you do that?

My dad. He didn't think that Mike would want me to mess up my exam schedule just to go to the funeral when I had already pretty much said goodbye at the funeral home.

So you didn't attend the funeral.

Nope. Never been to his grave either. Too busy attempting to be an obedient son and to please my father. A dangerous precedent that I fell into and didn't stop doing until I was long an adult myself.

I know.

Parenting should require some sort of licensing. I mean you need a license to drive a car, hunt wild animals, go fishing, but raising kids, anyone gets to do that.

What about David and Louis?

Oh, we got together several times, and even stayed in touch for about ten years while they were in various stages of graduate school and we were then moving all over the country pursuing our careers.

What did you talk about?

The guilt mostly.

Why did they feel guilty?

I felt guilty for abandoning all of them, and they felt guilty for not seeing how unhappy Mike had become, and for making their own plans to go away to college. It was a crazy time. Mike was an eccentric, and a talent. I often wonder if all talented people are not just a little off somehow as compensation for their brilliance.

Mike loved you.

I'm not sure of that. More than likely he probably felt like we - I – had abandoned him.

No. He knew you loved him. He said goodbye to you and David and Louis as well as his family.

How do you know that?

I was there.

And if you were there, then…

Yes. I was that prod you felt. I was that pang of conscience that you ignored. Don't feel bad. You weren't the first, and you won't be the last to ignore such a prompt. It remains my greatest frustration when people ignore what are truly gifts of the Spirit.

Oh good, more guilt.

That was not my intention.

For what it's worth, I have never ignored another prompting, no matter what it involved. I couldn't, I can't. I won't. Well, at least not for the rest of today, he said ruefully with a wan smile.

You have a full day ahead of you.

0715

"By failing to prepare, you are preparing to fail."
—Benjamin Franklin

Assuming that I am dying, what do I need to do today? I guess I should make sure that I assemble all of the important papers where I know that Kathy can find them. Over the next hour Jack pulled all the documents from their two safes in the garage and placed all the documents in a neat pile on his large oak desk in his study off the foyer. *Last Will and Testament of Jackson Davis Lee* read the long stuffed envelope. "I wonder how many people would question whether I am in my right mind today," he said to one of the dogs who looked curiously at him as he raised his head and then promptly lowered it back down into the deep cordovan red leather chair. "What do you think Bo, have I lost my marbles?" Again the dog looked at him with a look mixed with bewilderment and could it be, sadness, wondered Jack.

I guess that's it. Will, Trust, Power of Attorney, Health Care Power of Attorney with Living Will Provisions. "I guess you won't have to worry about making the decision of whether or not to pull the plug on me – I have it on good authority that I am checking out permanently today," he said to the large leather blotter that had covered his desk for more than thirty years.

It took only a few minutes more to organize the deeds to the house, the condo, the car titles, the appraisals and pictures on the art, jewelry, and collectible antique Colt pistols. "It's a shame that I can't take some of this stuff with me. I think I might miss a piece or two," he said grimly.

Checkbooks, Money Market passbooks, Certificates of Deposit, all nestled in the antique cigar box that he had been given by his grandfather oh so many years ago. They had thought about throwing it away so many times over the years, and now it was going to be around long after he was gone.

The Whole Life Insurance policies would keep Kathy and the kids very comfortable for a good many years. The idea that even the two smaller term life policies would be redeemed brought a small smile to his face. A friend of his from the Reserves had years ago cajoled him into supplementing his whole life insurance with a couple of smaller term policies. "Rich, I hate all insurance equally, but term insurance is such a rip-off. Ninety eight percent of them never pay off. You guys are bigger bloodsuckers than the casinos in Vegas," he had said as he accepted delivery and wrote the first of many checks. "Well, I guess I beat the House on this round," he said, placing the two policies on top of the two faux leather folders containing his permanent insurance.

Where did the time go? Guardians and Trustees for Bobby and Becky no longer needed, and now it is testamentary trusts for the grandkids in the event that his children precede him in death. Does not sound likely after today.

Where had the time gone? It seems like only yesterday that he was coaching Bobby in T-ball, and Becky in soccer. Of course there was that 'gap' where he was sort of checked out from their lives and was building a name for himself as a high priced defense attorney. The money had been very good, but the hours that he put in while in trial had been nothing short of grueling. If it were a local trial, he would often leave the house before the sun was up, and not come home until nearly the next day and the clock was chiming midnight. Birthdays, anniversaries, school functions, had been things he participated in via the memories captured on the camcorder.

Sounds like a regret Jack.

Yeah, maybe. But I went to law school to be an attorney, and being an attorney is what provided us with this house, the cars, and the condo in St. Pete, sent two kids to private college, and established modest trust funds for grandkids.

Would you do it again?

Would I do it again? Hmm. I don't know.

If you would do it again, would you do anything differently?

I guess I would not have worried as much about what others thought about me and the way I practiced law, or ran my unit in the Army, or how I conducted my real estate business.

What do you mean?

I mean my reputation was very important to me. But in hindsight I guess it would be a fair statement that most of us place way too much importance on what other people think about us. I remember how I used to dress a certain way for the jury depending on where the trial was taking place. I always felt as if I were on trial as well. How will they judge us? Or what did the neighbors think about the cars that were in our driveway. In the moment, we think their opinions are crucial to our future success and happiness.

And today?

In the big scheme of things, none of it really mattered. I mean we even pre-paid for our burial plots and my name is on a veteran's wall in a cemetery that I won't even be buried in, because we were caught up in the moment when we buried our good friend Ron about thirty years sooner than any of us thought we would. In a few days I am going to be in the ground, maybe in Hollywood Cemetery, and the best that I can hope for is that someone will come and pay their respects every now and again, but if Kathy remarries I don't expect her to do it, and with as busy as the kids and grandkids are, heck, I am going to become a distant memory.

Don't underestimate the impact you have made or the legacy you are leaving.

Oh yeah? What's going to become of the stuff that I have in boxes in the garage like my law degree and law licenses? Stuff from when I was a kid. Some of the stuff in our curio table that belonged to my grandparents? Not exactly choice Grade-A stuff for Craig's List. Will anyone hang on to it for a souvenir, or is it destined for the junk heap with all the other dust catchers? I sure hope someone hangs on to my Jackie Robinson baseball bat; I've had it since I was a kid.

Those pictures of your antique gun collection are quite nice.

Yeah, I really loved doing the research and finding the history attached to each piece. Some of them are museum quality.

I can see that. Do you have any favorites?

I guess this old M1911 Army .45 would be a favorite.

Why is that?

I remember the day it arrived from the Arsenal. I was seven years old. My dad paid $17.50 for it. I grew up shooting it, and when I was in ROTC my dad insisted that l be able to take it completely apart and reassemble it with my eyes closed while holding my breath.

Wasn't that a little extreme?

Some might say that. In his mind if that was going to be my personal sidearm when I went on active duty then by gum I was going to be able to take care of it.

Did you carry that on active duty?

Oh no. It stayed at home with him, but I carried an M1911A1 which is exactly the same. When I came home and went into the Reserves I would use it for annual qualification and the like.

It's nice that you have it now. When did your dad give it to you?

Give it to me? That's funny. A good bit of these guns that I acquired from him were in lieu of payment for legal services rendered. A few of them, like this one, indicating a gold and ivory decorated one, he sold to me at what he had paid for it.

How did you acquire the .45 that you favor so much?

Well, my dad liquidated his collection largely without telling me, and gave one of my brothers a few of the guns to include this one. When I went looking for it and learned that he had it, I was very angry, disappointed, and hurt.

So your brother gave it to you then?

Oh no, he sold it to me along with another gun that my dad had given him. He needed the money and was going to sell it on e-Bay if I did not buy it from him.

Oh my.

It was my dad's way.

What do you mean?

When his father died, my grandmother did not have a driver's license, had no need for their car, and *gave* it to my Dad. Two years later when I was old enough to drive, he *sold it* to me for $200. Cash on the barrel head.

I just want my kids to appreciate my stuff, and if they don't want it, to put it museums or wherever it is going to do some good. I don't want it languishing in a pawn shop.

Are your concerns really about your material objects or is it something more that is troubling you Jack?

Yeah, he started. There is more. Is anyone even going to remember that I lived? I mean, sure, my kids will remember that I was their dad, and hopefully will think of me on father's day, and maybe my birthday. But are they going to think about me at other times?

Of course they will.

I'd like to think so, but how can I compete with Google?

What do you mean?

When they were kids, it was "hey Dad, what time is it? Hey Dad, how do you spell Cincinnati?" Now, it's just a click away on their phone.

Are you afraid that they won't remember what you taught them?

Not necessarily, but it would be nice to have them pass on some of the things that I taught them to their kids and say something like, "when I was a kid, your grandpa Jack taught me 'measure twice, cut once,' in such a way that I will never forget it, and hope that you won't ever forget it either," said Jack.

Don't underestimate the lessons you taught or whether they heard you.

Sometimes I used to wonder if they were listening at all.

They were listening Jack, and they will forever hear your voice in their hearts.

I want them to be happy, but to miss me too. I always thought that I would be around for a lot of years and see my grandchildren graduate college, having babies, and being that crazy old man that made the kids laugh when I pulled quarters out of their ears, he said, wiping a tear from the corner of each eye before they fell on to the papers neatly stacked on the desk.

Were you happy Jack?

Overall I think I was.

When were you not happy?

When I did not have confidence in myself.

Jack, you graduated cum laude from undergraduate, and did well in all of your army schools.

I know, but when I got to law school, a lot of doubts crept back into my belfry. The first day of class the dean made a point of congratulating us on being accepted into law school and then cut the legs out from under us when he pointed out that 'ninety percent of you can no longer be in the top ten percent.'

Why did that bother you?

It was shades of my dad all over again. In his zeal to make me the perfect one by keeping my feet in the fire, he instilled a great fear of failure in me that exists in some small part even to this day.

Really. I never would have thought that of you. You passed the bar exam, and all of the other exams that you have ever taken.

But never first without the fear running through my mind of 'what if I don't pass this test?' I even worry when I do my continuing education!

I'm sorry that you have had to live like that.

Oh yeah. Every home repair that I do around here always starts with, 'what if screw this up?'

And what if you do?

Well now, I don't care. If I fix it or install it correctly, I get the double joy of saving the money and having done it myself.

And if you mess it up?

Then I call someone to fix it. But you know what, that does not happen very often. I learned a lot from my dad, and I am a pretty smart guy, so I can do most of the things that I set my mind to doing.

That was quite a burden to carry.

Don't I know it! That is why I just want my kids to be the best that they can be, and to be happy with their best efforts.

I believe that you have bestowed a wonderful gift on your children because you did not burden them with these same fears and concerns that have weighed so heavily on your shoulders, often intruding on your own beliefs and undermining your self-confidence. I don't think it was your father's intention to do this to you.

I don't think it was either, but the scars are there, and it wasn't until I changed careers that I finally found myself free of seeking his approval. I found that my self-esteem and self-worth were too so tied up in the approval that I either received or did not receive.

Jack, self-esteem is how we see ourselves through the eyes of the world. There are times when our self-esteem will take a beating because the world can be a very harsh place. Self-worth is something completely different. Your self-worth is how your Heavenly Father sees you as one of His children, and in His eyes, your worth is infinite.

That's pretty profound stuff for eight o'clock in the morning,

It is something that you have always known, but never acknowledged to yourself.

0820

"The thing to do, it seems to me, is to prepare yourself so you can be a rainbow in somebody else's cloud. Somebody who may not look like you. May not call God the same name you call God - if they call God at all. I may not dance your dances or speak your language. But be a blessing to somebody. That's what I think."

—Maya Angelou

This is crazy. I feel fine. My heart threw me a *twinge* is all. So what? I didn't have any pain in my left arm, didn't feel woozy or any anything. I am probably imagining all of this.

You are *going to die today Jack.*

Says who? I am not going to die today. This is all a hallucination of some kind.

Denial is a step in the process that you can ill afford.

How about anger then?

No, you don't get to enjoy that emotion either, unless you want the gift taken away.

Knowing that I am going to die is considered a *gift?*

Very much so. Can you imagine how many people would give all that they possessed simply for another last day? Another last day in which to make amends, right wrongs, say effective goodbyes, to impart wisdom and to insure that the legacy they leave behind is in order? Look at what you have already accomplished this morning by getting everything so neatly organized on your desk. Why did you do that as opposed to having another cup of coffee and reading the newspaper?

Because it was the right thing to do. It is going to be hard enough for Kathy and the kids when I check out prematurely; having everything organized just makes things a little easier for all concerned.

Any other reasons you took these steps?

Because I love them, and don't want them to experience any undue frustration or concerns.

Exactly. So now the question is what else should you do today to insure that everything is in order, all is where it should be, and that you can leave with me later with a clear mind and a light heart?

What do you mean?

Have you and Kathy ever talked about what kind of funeral each of you might want, and put together any details?

Not in total detail, but I think she knows that I want a military funeral like we gave my buddy years ago.

Write it down right now. Think about who you would like to speak at your funeral and where you would like to have it take place. Deciding some of these things and putting your family in the position of 'honoring your wishes' is another burden that you can take off of their shoulders and ease some of their pain.

I never thought of that.

I have escorted people who have even written their own obituaries.

That's kind of morbid I think. Or the ultimate in micro-management.

Or just an attempt to let people know what was in your heart and to help them remember more of your virtues.

I never thought of it that way.

Haven't you ever been surprised at how well someone you only casually know seems to know you as well as you know yourself?

I've got that!

Excuse me? What do you mean that you have that?

As part of a leadership retreat I participated in a couple of years ago with my real estate brokerage, they had us all draft our "Final Words: Value Statement," as an exercise intended to make us see ourselves. After we submitted it to the group, the group then got to take a crack at it and essentially write it up in final form.

You sound dubious of the exercise.

Not at all. While at first I felt like I was writing my own obituary, I actually got into it, and spent a good bit of time on it overnight when it was assigned as homework. I found it very interesting to see what the class then did to it and how they viewed me very similarly to the way that I view myself. It was actually voted 'best in class.'

Do you know where it is?

Actually I do. I've always kept it with my legal papers, he said, his voice trailing off. Here it is…

Jackson Davis Lee was a loving teacher and example of simple truths, whose sense of right and wrong was as defined as black and white. There was no gray, for this reason one always could predict the answer to any situation with which Jack found himself confronted. His leadership helped people find the best within themselves and to recognize the distinction between the God-provided self-worth, and the world's evaluation of us that we find in our self-esteem. His leadership was such that it made us believe in ourselves, in a selfless vision, and to want to achieve more not only for ourselves but for those around us, because there is no 'I' in the word Team.

He was a caring and loving child of God, husband, father, grandfather, son, brother, father-in-law, brother-in-law, uncle, cousin, friend, business colleague, Army officer, Scouter, packrat, and quintessential saver who strove to find balance between success and significance. He had an inner spiritual peace about him that permitted him to say no in a loving manner to people and projects that got him off purpose.

He was a person of high energy who was able to see the positive in any event or situation. Possessing an achievement drive higher than most, he offset an admitted lack of talent with a seemingly infinite source of energy and hard work. With his eyes to the horizon, he saw beyond the immediate obstacles. A man of vision, he always had a plan for himself, his family, and for his business. No matter what happened, he could find a 'learning' or message in it. He believed without seeing, and as he grew older enjoyed more and more the simple pleasures of life derived from being a member of an eternal family. His faith was simple – almost child-like, his knowledge of the scriptures rudimentary, but his knowledge of the worlds to come immense because of years and years spent in service to others.

A voracious reader, he never wanted to stop learning, and was proud of his academic and professional credentials, as well as his military awards and decorations, without wearing them on his sleeve. He enjoyed traveling and doing things that he had only read about as a young man. Not into material things himself, he was a hard person to buy a gift for, but always generous when it came to his family and friends.

He valued integrity to such a high degree, that he insured that his actions were consistent with his words, and he was always striving to be an example and to be the best, all the while without imposing his will or desire on other people. While not an Eagle Scout himself, he lived the ideals of Scouting.

He will be missed because wherever he went, he made the world a better place by his having been there. He believed that there are no small acts of kindness, and that being Christ-like means always saying thank you and encouraging the heart. For this reason he never forgot a kind deed done to him, and tried to personify the legend of the Starfish by making the difference one life at a time.

He lived his life in congruence with his values, by modeling the way, by challenging the process when necessary, by always remembering his roots and heritage, and never straying one degree from his True North of Family, Duty, and Honor.

I think that captures the essence of who you are. Do you?

Sometimes. As we talked about earlier, sometimes I know that I placed way too much importance on what other people around me thought about what I was doing. I became an attorney because it was what everyone thought I was suited to do with my life.

What would you have preferred to do?

I don't know. I thought about staying in the Army. Thought about being a dentist when I was a teenager, but never got any real guidance on it. Ironically, years later when I mentioned this to our family dentist for whom I was by then swapping dental services for legal services, he said that had he known of my desire to be a dentist, he would have seen to it that I became a dentist and would probably be his partner at this point.

Fascinating.

You sound like Mr. Spock.

A very creative mind Gene Roddenberry.

Relating to a previous point, a big regret is why despite all my successes, I still labored with such little confidence in myself. I can still remember coming home with five A's and one B on a report card and the focus would be on the lone B. It really messed with my mind. The harshest words my father could throw at me were "I am disappointed." They were enough to crush me. It actually angers me that I allowed him and others to have such power over me. It genuinely made me think poorly of myself.

What was your greatest talent?

Well, it certainly was not being musical or artistic. Even though I won a scholastic art award in 8th grade, it was for abstract art. I don't play an instrument, but it is on my bucket list. Oh. No more bucket list.

You don't need a bucket list in Heaven. You'll discover talents that you never knew to be in your possession.

Well don't look for me to be a singing angel or anything, because I can't carry a tune in a bucket. My daughter Becky made me so self-conscious about my voice that I won't sing when I am around her, even if at church. Kathy says that I have a good voice but simply don't know what to do with it. I think I sound okay in the shower.

In Heaven there is a lot of singing. Joyful singing as we bask in the glow of the light, said the Spirit preceded by a short laugh.

I didn't know that spirits laughed.

Heaven is a happy place Jack. Light. Laugher, Love.

Sounds wonderful.

So what was your greatest talent?

Oh. I worked the hardest. I took pride in the fact that I would take the longest most circuitous route, carrying the heaviest pack, intent on getting there first in the fastest time, with the most in tow.

What did that mean in your life?

It meant graduating college in less than three years, being commissioned at age nineteen, all the while juggling 24 credit hours each quarter, working a full-time and part-time job and being self-sufficient since I was age 14.

What did it mean for others? That is what Heaven is all about. Others.

I, uh, don't know. I mean it made me independent and self-reliant, and not a burden on anyone. It made me stronger, tougher, and able to take whatever Life dished out my way I guess.

Would you do it again?

Aside from the things I missed out on like being there for Mike, or finishing my Eagle Scout award, and some of the other 'kid' stuff that I missed out on, I think I would. I think it made me the person that I am today. I hope the decisions that I made as a parent were good ones and that I didn't mess up my kids like my parents messed me up. The most frequently made observation that Kathy has made over the years is that she marvels at how 'normal' I turned out despite my upbringing.

Nothing you did could have changed anything in terms of Mike you know.

Ah, but that is forty years of twenty-twenty hindsight speaking. Guilt is a wonderful thing. Just ask my mother or either of my grandmothers, they raised it to an art form.

Being angry and blaming yourself for not being able to control the past much less anything that can or will occur in the future is only going to hurt you worse. That is not what Heaven is about. While everything has to have its opposite, guilt is decidedly something that we don't even address in Heaven. If you keep thinking like this, you will only be re-inventing pain for yourself and those around you.

So you just don't think about it? You don't address it? You ignore it? What's the deal?

One of the reasons you come to Earth is to gain experiences that are not available in Heaven. It is where you experience those opposites that we were just talking about. In life you find pleasure. In life you find pain. Pleasure and pain is an example of the duality in life.

Why do they both have to exist?

It is only through this duality that we can truly grasp all that life has to offer. If we never tasted sorrow, we would not appreciate joy. Enjoy them both, for they are an intertwined part of the experience. The key is to not turn the pain into something else: regret.

0940

"The fruit of the righteous is a tree of life;
and he that winneth souls is wise."
—Proverbs 11:30

We still have a good bit of the day to accomplish a great deal of work. Have you thought about what you want your legacy to be after you are gone?

When the first Gulf War came along years ago, it changed life for everyone who was wearing the green on the weekend. It used to be that most guys could count on one weekend a month and two weeks in the summer, and that was it.

That wasn't your experience?

Nothing even close to it. Some of it was the fact that I was an officer, and some of it was the nature of the assignments that I was in. Couple that with the fact the higher rank you are, the harder it is to 'hide' and you end up like I did, averaging two to two and a half weekends, and a lot more than just two weeks.

Regrets?

Sometimes, for the time it took me away from the family, but while I was doing it, I felt as if I was answering a higher call. Not everyone is equipped to be in the military, and truth be told, I was pretty good at what I did.

So it was a calling of sorts for you?

For me, it certainly was. I was proud to wear the uniform of my country and to serve in the same manner that my two uncles had done during World War II.

So only a mild regret.

Yeah.

So what do you want your legacy to be is the question of the moment.

Oh yeah, sorry. As I was saying, when the first Gulf War came along, I was a brand new major, assigned to the general staff in an armored training division. We were waiting for our mobilization orders that would take us down to Fort Bliss, TX where our general would become the post commander, and we would backfill all the units on post that were heading over to the sandbox. I also realized that being an *artillery* officer in an armored unit was going to make me stick out like sore thumb and that if there was an artillery unit somewhere that needed a battalion executive officer, I was probably heading over to the sand box as well.

Were you afraid to do that?

Not afraid, but concerned about what the interruption would mean to my family life. I mean who was going to teach my kids the things they needed to learn? I wasn't afraid of getting killed or anything, but just missing out on teaching them the really important stuff.

Such as?

Well, first and foremost, you can't grow up in the Lee family without hearing a whole lot about honoring our family name, doing right by the Commonwealth, and the United States now that we are one again, and never failing in our duty. Until the day she died, my grandmother drilled it into us that we should never ever do anything that would tarnish the Lee family name.

And you've lived that from what I have observed.

I would like to think so.

So what happened with the war?

As luck would have it, the ground war only lasted less than 100 hours, the president said 'we're done,' and I did not have to deploy.

How did that make you feel?

I don't think it made me feel one way or another. I was glad that I didn't have to go, disrupt my legal practice and my family life, but had I been called upon, I would have gone willingly.

So what have you taught your children?

Well, just like a close call at the doctor's office will cause you to change your lifestyle, this little episode with Desert Storm, got me to seriously contemplate what I wanted to leave as a template for my children to learn from in the event that something ever did happen to me.

And?

I ran across this book called *Eight Points of the Compass* and discovered that the author was a guy just like me who had faced the same dilemma when the balloon went up over the desert, but he did something about it.

What did he do?

Some years later he actually sat down and wrote a book for his kids and his grandkids. He too had figured out that he needed to leave something behind for everyone to follow.

And what impressed you with this book?

First and foremost that we shared a common True North.

That being…

True North has been and always will be, thanks to Grammy Lee, all about Integrity. Without it, you have absolutely nothing. There is a quote in the book that essentially says 'thoughts lead to purpose, purpose leads to actions, actions form habits, habits decide character, and Character fixes our destiny.'

Your character does fix your destiny. It is the only thing that you take with you from your earthly probation. What else impressed you in the book?

That you have to live your life with an attitude of gratitude. There are always going to be people who have more than you, but there will be even more people who have less than you. The choice you need to make is to be grateful for all that you do have, and not regret that which you don't.

You can't change the wind, but you can adjust the sails.

Exactly. It is all about choosing our attitude.

Beyond a doubt, charity and generosity really are gifts that we give to ourselves.

I also took away the importance of maintaining balance and equilibrium between the tracks of our life.

Elaborate please.

While I was practicing law there were too many times that my life was out of balance. Just as you can't serve two masters, it is impossible to give 110% to everything before you start failing at everything. Focus on everything eventually becomes focus on nothing.

It's hard to learn from a mistake you don't acknowledge.

It's the main reason that I finally gave up practicing law. I knew that I had messed up with my kids, and figured having grandkids was a mighty 'do over' on which I was not going to lose out.

No other success can compensate for failure in the home.

I am just grateful that I didn't screw up bad enough that I had a kid who turned to drugs, or crime, or really strayed from the straight and narrow.

You have wonderful kids. You and Kathy did a fine job.

Well, I know that it was mainly Kathy, because I was gone a lot more than I ever contemplated being.

Learn from the past, plan for the future, but live in the present.

I don't have a future any more after today....

What else did you take away from the book?

That it is all about commitment. Whatever you do, commit to it. Don't do anything half-baked. You sure wouldn't want to be treated by a doctor who only went to class half the time. There was a quote in the book that said, "Make your life a mission, not an intermission."

Well said.

I also had a bit of an epiphany while reading this book when I learned that life is about abundance.

Explain.

Wealth is more than money. That it is about your character and what you *do* in life and not about who accumulates the most toys.

Benjamin Franklin once said, 'if your riches are yours, why don't you take them with you to the other World?'

Exactly the point. It changed me. I stopped worrying as much about billable hours and started spending more time with the family. That was the year that I became Bobby's little league coach. It was also the time that I started to seriously craft the vision of what I wanted the rest of my life to be, and what I wanted to accomplish as my own version of being a renaissance man.

You become what you think about most of the time.

Now that's profound.

Ralph Waldo Emerson. Remember, I've met all of the great ones.

I never thought of that. What's that like?

You'll find out. What else did you learn from this book?

That Life is all about relationships, keeping commitments to others, and being there for others. Forming and maintaining these relationships require us to be committed and to do exactly the same thing whether or not someone is watching us.

No cases of eyestrain have been developed by looking on the bright side of things.

I like that. Who said it?

You can now. It was anonymous.

1100

"Don't count the days, make the days count."
—Muhammed Ali

Okay, you have convinced me. I am really going to die today. I guess I need to start saying goodbye...

No goodbyes Jack. That vitiates the gift. You can say and do anything you want to do with anyone around you, but you can't tell them that you are dying.

What? What kind of gift is it if it comes with strings attached?

Still a gift. Seek joy in what you give, not in what you get.

Still a quote machine I see.

Most escorts have found that it is easier to teach their charges through the use of quotes and parables, and with things familiar.

Familiarity sometimes breeds contempt you know.

Call your brother Jack.

I hope I catch him when he can talk. I never know his schedule; it is sometimes pretty hit and miss.

Call your brother.

I guess if I don't get him now, I can always leave a message and try again tomorrow.

Nice try Jack. Dial.

Johnston Pickett Lee is two years younger than Jack, and was named for both Generals Sydney Albert Johnston and George Pickett. As young children they were largely inseparable until their father determined that he had very definitive plans for eldest son Jackson.

"Hello," said Johnny, sounding distracted.

"Hey Johnny, its Jack."

"Jackie! How are you boy?"

"Good. Good. How 'bout you?"

"Oh same old, same old."

"How's your arm doing?"

"Oh a little sore if I overdo it, but the boss is giving me some lighter assignments, so I can't complain too much."

"Are you at work now?"

"Yeah, but you must be having me watched, because I literally went on break like thirty seconds ago, and just grabbed some sweet tea. What's up?"

"Nothing is up. I was just thinking about my first baby brother, and thought I would call you."

"Do tell."

"Actually, I was staring at the picture of you and me on our toy orange tractor. Can that picture really be more than fifty years old?"

"Yeah, that was a long time ago."

"Simpler times. Remember how we would go outside and play for hours?"

"Did we have a choice? Mom would feed us lunch and then lock us out of the house until Dad came home from work and she had to let us in for dinner."

"That's true," said Jack with a chuckle.

"But we still had fun."

"Yes we did," said Jack with his voice trailing off.

"So what's up with you? How's Kath and the kids?"

"They're great, and doing well. I am amazed at how fast their kids are growing up now."

"Ain't that the truth!"

"You know Johnny, you are a good man. I have always admired the size of your heart."

"Well there's a thought from left field. What's with the heavy thoughts today?"

"Nothing. I was working from home today, decided to do a little cleaning, was dusting the shelves in my study, saw that stupid picture of us together, and figured I would call and simply see how you are doing."

"To be honest, work is hard, and getting harder, and I don't know how much longer I can hold on. We aren't kids any more Jackie boy. But, the kids are great, and I am looking forward to a vacation next week and I get to see a couple of the kids and some of the grandkids, so I am not going to complain. Don't want the good Lord to send a lightning bolt my way for being an ingrate."

"Don't I know it." *I'll be on vacation next week too...permanently.* "Well enjoy your time off, you certainly deserve it. They are all lucky to have you Johnny. I am glad that we got to grow up together."

"Me too, I think."

"Oh yeah. Sorry about the mud," as he imagined the episode from their childhood to which his brother could be alluding.

"Mud my eye. That was certifiable dog crap that you had me pick up barehanded when we were building a dam in the curb of the street," said Johnny with a snort.

"Indeed it was," said Jack with a chuckle, as a tear escaped his right eye as he remembered the incident as if it were yesterday.

"But you saved my life by jumping in the pool up at Brown's Lake when we were real little and you couldn't even swim yourself."

"I wasn't thinking. I just saw you going down for the third time, and figured I would get blamed if you drowned, so I jumped in."

"And nearly drowned."

"I was close enough to the side of the pool that I figured I could save us both."

"Of course you got me in trouble when we broke the lamp together, and you threw me under the bus."

"They would have crucified me after my breaking the porch light on your head," said Jack.

"But you made up for it when you saved my life in the swamp," replied Johnny.

"But we nearly lost your cowboy boots. Good thing that they cleaned up."

"Somebody was sure watching out for us when we were pulling some pretty knuckleheaded stunts."

"Speaking of knuckleheaded stunts, I'm sorry for breaking your arm too," said Jack with a catch in his voice.

"Who knew that a teeter totter could be so dangerous, right?" said his brother.

"Still. I feel bad that because I jumped off, you busted your arm."

"Hey, you signed my cast, and as I remember, you had to do all my chores while I had the cast on my arm, so I think we are even."

"Thanks for being my brother," said Jack.

"I really didn't have a choice, did I?"

"No, you didn't. But I know that it was not always easy for you, especially when the old man would compare our report cards and crap like that."

"Hey, you weren't doing anything wrong."

"We had fun didn't we," asked Jack.

"Yeah we did. And hey, I owe you a lot. You taught me how to ride a two-wheeler. That could be huge if I decide to retire and become a bicycle messenger down in Florida," said Johnny with a chuckle.

"Sounds like a plan. Maybe I'll join you."

"It could be Lee Enterprises all over again," referring to a club that they had formed when they were young boys.

"There you go. This time we'll organize it with preferred stock too."

"Yeah, whatever. Hey, my break is over, and I got to get back on the floor. Thanks for calling."

"I love you Johnny."

"Love you too Jackie."

"Like a brother," they said in unison.

Silence.

That was nice. How do you feel?

Like bawling.

Why?

I never realized *not* saying goodbye would be so hard.

Isn't it still better than the alternative?

Yes, I guess it is.

I had forgotten that you saved your brother's life twice.

Well, maybe once in the pool. But certainly someone would have spotted him under the water with that red hair of his.

Somebody did. You. You jumped right in without even a thought to your own safety, and a non-swimmer to boot.

I don't know what you want me to say.

You don't have to say anything. Greater love has no one than this; that someone lay down his life for his friends.

John 15:13.

Good, you know it.

When did you finally learn how to swim?

Ha, ha, ha. I swim like a rock.

But you learned at some point.

Yeah, you could say that. My parents had a friendship with another couple (my dad and he worked together professionally) with a family comprised mostly of girls of corresponding ages to my brothers and I. One year when I was about twelve years old, we took a vacation together and I remember being challenged by my dad's co-worker to jump into the deep end of the motel pool at which we were staying. When I balked at the idea of jumping into water well over my head — it was deep enough to warrant a diving board — my dad's friend took it upon himself to throw me in the pool with no warning or time for either physical or mental preparation on my part.

Oh my. Talk about baptism by fire. Or I guess this would be full immersion.

Cute. In any event, I remember the sensation of sinking, hitting the bottom of the pool, the pressure and rush of noise in my ears, water in my nose, and the sheer terror and fear of drowning. I remember the sensation of opening my eyes, and not being able to see since my very fashionable thick black framed glasses had come off my face and were resting on the floor of the pool, seeing the light thru the water, and kicking off the bottom and "going towards the light" above. When I broke the surface kicking with my legs, thrashing my arms, and coughing to clear my lungs, I was aware of my pounding heart, and how anger was replacing the emotion of fear. When I finally found my voice and asked both Dick and my dad, "weren't you afraid that I might drown?" Dick was quick to answer with a chuckle, "Naw, because turds float." Had I been about two feet taller and 150 pounds heavier, I might have taken a swing at the guy.

Ironically, Dick's wife was more upset (if not darn right furious) with his actions than was my own mother. As I recall, my father who was standing next to Dick when he grabbed me, thought "it was time that I learned how to swim, and necessity was a good teacher."

What effect do you think that had on the rest of your life?

I figured out as a twelve year old that fear, anger, and humiliation are powerful emotions, better left buried. When so brutally exposed, they can be debilitating for some people. While this was not the case for me, I do remember vowing to myself at that moment in time that I would never knowingly or intentionally subject anyone that I knew — family, friends, or people that I would eventually lead or work with — to those emotions by virtue of any action on my part. It was truly a defining moment in the person that I would become. Some forty five years later I remember that moment and that resolution made, and have attempted to live by it with my children, my troops, and all other followers.

What other effect did this experience have on you?

Fear of drowning aside, I do look back on that experience with mixed emotions. While it did not make me a swimmer, or vitiate my already healthy respect for water, it did foster the heretofore referenced resolution on what I would never inflict on another human being, and also created a resolve in me to stretch beyond my limits and to in fact get outside of my comfort zone and not allow fear to debilitate me. This resolution allowed me to embrace things like rappelling down the sides of high rise buildings in downtown Richmond (I even have a headline picture of me doing it captured by the *Richmond Times*) and out of helicopters, to go skydiving, and imbued me with the ability to make decisions at the early stages of my professional work life which prompted superiors to notice me and to promote me with regularity. As it is my habit to look for silver linings, I am attributing the foregoing to my less than delightful water experience.

As a bit of an epilogue I should note that while I have maintained my very healthy respect for all water, but particularly the ocean, I have not allowed it to stop me from experiencing life. While we were on an incentive trip with my company to Australia and Hayman Island, we were presented with the once-in-a-lifetime opportunity to snorkel the Great Barrier Reef off of Australia. While I was a little reticent about doing so – it involves water – I have always loved fish and knew that I would kick myself for the rest of my life if I did not take advantage of this opportunity. I also was willing to do this because I knew what to do to remain safe and to maximize the experience. I had learned in the Boy Scouts that we never ever swim without a "swim buddy." Heck, even U.S. Navy SEALs utilize the system of swim buddies. As you probably guessed, my swim buddy for this adventure was going to be the very mermaid to whom I am wed.

Well, I was in fact immediately abandoned by my beloved "swim buddy" –literally in the first forty seconds that we were in the water together – because she immediately "forgot about me as soon as she hit the water because of all there was to see," — but that was okay because after an hour in the water, I had witnessed fish and sea life beyond my wildest imagination. I was then able to mosey back to the mini-yacht we were on for the day and to enjoy the vast buffet of goodies that had been catered for us while she spent another two hours in the water.

That is quite a story.
The absolute truth I assure you.

You know, I have been thinking about what you have shared with me today. May I share some observations?

My time is your time….seemingly forever and ever now.

You have a very great capacity for love Jackson Davis Lee. I think you have underestimated the life you have led. There is a great deal of Heaven already in your heart.

My heart is aching right now.

As it should be; Transition day is often difficult.

If you weren't a heavenly being, I might use some language from my rough and tumble army days to describe just how *difficult* this whole concept is to imagine, much less embrace.

No need for that, we have Georgie Patton who still does that some seventy years after his transition day. It still astounds many of us how such a pious, God-fearing, articulate, and well-read man, can conjure up words and whole sentences that are so visceral.

Does he slap the other angels or has he learned to play well with others? The word anathema comes to mind.

No, he does not slap anyone. We know that Georgie has a good heart. When he forgets himself and goes too far afield, we just ask Omar Bradley to take him under his wing and administer a little love. Remember it's all about light, love and laughter.

Sounds like you have it all figured out.

I don't have anything figured out. It's simply Heaven's Code. You'll come to appreciate it as well.

Couldn't I figure it out in about forty more years?

Call your brother.

1155

"The beauty of life does not depend on how happy you are,
But how happy others can be because of you."
—Unknown

"Hey Chick, its Jack."

"You mean I have a brother?" said James Hill Lee in a falsetto voice. Named for Confederate generals James Longstreet and A.P. Hill, Jimmy now lives in Texas. At eight years younger than Jackson, he is very aware of his own fiftieth birthday that is looming on the horizon.

"Yes, you have a brother," replied Jack, carrying on a tradition that had been going on for many years.

"How are you? How's Kath and the kids?"

"All doing well. How's your brood?"

"No complaints. Life is very good. The kids visited last weekend, we spent the whole time in the hot tub and pool in the backyard. We watched movies on a sheet that I stretched across the deck, and we had an absolute blast," said Jimmy with enthusiasm.

"That's awesome. You really do have a nice little playground down there."

"It's a totally different standard of living when you live in the middle of nowhere. Who would have thought that I could give up the big house, the artwork, and fancy car and jewelry, and be genuinely happier than I have ever been?"

"Proud of you little brother," said Jack.

"Well, that means a lot Jackie. I know that I didn't always do things that made the family proud of me."

"Hey, you were a punk kid, and ran with the wrong crowd for a little while."

"You never gave up on me though."

"Let's just say that I saw the potential when nobody else did," said Jack lightly.

"I've never forgotten it."

"You'll always be my baby brother," said Jack.

"I know. And believe it or not, I have always appreciated that. Especially when you sort of had to take charge of the family."

"You do what you gotta do for the people you love."

"Hey, have you done any fishing lately?" asked Jimmy, flitting to another topic as he is apt to do.

"No. I want to, but I've been busy, and we've been doing stuff with the grandkids."

"Well, the fish will be biting on the Chickahominy in the next few weeks. Do me a favor and catch a few for me."

"I surely will."

"Hey, you know what I did last week?"

"No what?"

"I taught my granddaughter how to ride a two-wheeler, and immediately thought of you."

"Hey, that's cool."

"Don't you remember, you taught me how to ride a two wheeler on the same day that you taught Johnny," he said with a laugh at the recollection.

"I remember, trust me. You were a lot easier to teach than Johnny."

"I think the only reason he finally learned was to shut you up," said Jimmy.

"It made us into the Three Musketeers once we all had wheels," recalled Jack.

"You know it. But you were always there for me. You taught me how to catch and throw a baseball, and you also beat those kids up who pulled me off my bike in the middle of the street."

"Oh yeah. I haven't thought about that in years. I have never been as angry as I was that day. Nobody gets to beat up my little brother except me," said Jack.

"You became my hero that day Jackie," said his younger brother. "I knew that I never needed to be afraid again, because I had a big brother looking out for me."

"That's what big brothers do, you know?"

"Yeah, but you went above and beyond. I was a punk in high school and I just remember you coming home on leave in your Army uniform and threatening to beat on me if I didn't ditch the loser friends and get my act together."

"Hey, you got involved with the wrong group of friends, and we do dumb stuff when we're young. We're impressionable. Let's face it, with Mom and Dad splitting up, you didn't exactly have the best role models around, much less any real supervision. It didn't surprise me that you made friends with the wrong crowd. They were your friends and you thought that they really cared about you. At least you got out before you did something dumb that landed you in jail or dead."

"You were there for me, and that made the difference."

"Pay it forward little brother, pay it forward."

"So what's going on with you these days?" asked Jimmy.

"Same old same old. The kids were over last weekend, and we had a great time until one of them 'grounded me from talking,' at the kitchen table during dinner."

"Why would they do that to you," asked Jimmy with a trace of mirth in his voice.

"For some reason they think they have the right to accuse me of being too much of a storyteller, and that I tell the same stories and same jokes over and over."

"You are, and you do. That's what we count on from you Jackie," teased his brother.

"I have resolved that the solution is to keep the old material and to continue to find new audiences."

"How's that working for you guy?" asked his brother.

"Actually pretty well. My real estate clients, the other brokers, the title company folks, they all laugh at all my jokes," said Jack.

"Great. At least you have a new generation of grandkids to torture now," he teased.

"I also resolved that I am going to prove that you were all wrong for giving me such a hard time."

"Oh yeah, how are you going to do that wise guy?" asked his brother.

"Here's how it is going to go down. See, I am going to outlive all of you even though I am the oldest because I have been the one who led the clean life, didn't drink or smoke, and was the best looking to boot."

"Is that medication talking, or are you hallucinating?" he asked, interrupting his brother's story.

"Listen up. You, Johnny and Jujube are going to be sitting in Heaven, wondering what to do until I show up."

"Uh huh. And then," he asked.

"We're gonna be sitting down under the trees near the dock with the Man himself, and I am going to tell Him all of my jokes, and all of my stories. And He is going to say, 'you're right,' and 'that's really funny.' Now think about it for a minute. God is everywhere all the time, and so He's heard me tell the stories before hundreds of times. Rather than give me a hard time, He'll remind me of the parts I forgot or maybe embellished too much, and naturally highlight the parts that were His favorite. Then He will turn to you guys, call you losers, and ask you why you can't be half as witty as me," said Jack.

"Oh yeah. I can see that."

"P.S. If you were half as witty as me that would make you a half-wit."

"Saw that one coming Jackie. You are getting predictable in your old age."

"Old age? I don't think so birthday boy. I don't take any meds and someone on this call is staring the big 5-0 in the face on his next birthday. Any time you want to mix it up, let me know because I can still take you."

"Never doubt it for a minute," said his brother.

"There you go again Chick," said Jack.

"What?"

"Doing what you do best. You were always Switzerland in the family. Completely neutral and always playing the Peacemaker."

"Hey, you got the brains, and I am good at fixing things that are broken from things around the house to matters of the heart. Let's face it shyster that is why you were so good at being an attorney. Quick with a story, quick on your feet, and a rapier like wit. I on the other hand, smooth ruffled feathers, and can work with my hands. Did I tell you that I just replaced my own hot water heater?"

"No. Wow. No way I go near welding and plumbing on that scale. But, I don't think we are all that different. Dad insisted all of us get fairly handy around the house. I just re-tiled all the backsplashes in the kitchen for Kathy, and I gotta say, it looks pretty darn good."

"Well good. A little *manual labor* is good for the soul," said Jimmy, "especially for you book smart fellers who need a reminder of what it is like to work with your hands."

"And truth be told, I know that you are a smart guy. It may have taken you longer to learn some of the lessons that I already had learned at a much younger age, but you mastered them."

"How so?"

"Let's face it, for a long time, you made it, and you spent it. And we were talking some serious bucks at a couple points of your career. But it was all about your stuff…and what it cost."

"That's true, that's true."

"Part of me really hated it when you were making big bucks and living large because I was afraid that it could all stop, and if it did, that you might not be able to handle the change that accompanied it. We would come over to your house and it would be like visiting Mom as you had to play show and tell, and do everything but put a price tag on the picture frame for all of us to see."

"And then it stopped."

"Yes it did. But you didn't. A lesser man might have let it knock him to the canvas, but rather than stopping yourself, you took stock, and with your out loud voice acknowledged that not having a degree was going to make it tough, but that you were going to move on. You then found yourself a new niche, and you are doing great, and I could not be prouder of you," said Jack.

"That means a lot to hear Jackie," said Jimmy.

"I believe it was then that you found yourself. You became comfortable in your own skin and it became less about the money and trappings associated with wealth, and more about abundance rather than out and out money."

"That's true."

"I remember just a few years ago when I turned 50 and said that I was halfway there, you thought it was outrageous that I wanted to live to be a hundred and you went so far as to say that if you lived as long as dad did to age 69 that you would be satisfied."

"I just could not imagine working that long, or what I would do if I was not working, and what would fill all that time up."

"Now it is all about your family, and that is what Heaven's Code is all about.

You are going to be great, for a long long time to come. Now you live very providently, you avoid debt, and you are focused on your kids and grandkids. You have the light of heaven in your heart. I am so proud of the man that you have become," said Jack.

"To tell you the truth, I always wanted to be like you. It just took me longer to figure out how to do it," said Jimmy.

"Well Chick, you may have been born on Thanksgiving and been called the Turkey Kid, but you will forever be the Chicken Boy to me," said Jack, making reference to the time when a then four year old Jimmy had asked if the man who worked with their grandfather was going to keep calling him the chicken boy.

"Hey Jackie, thanks for calling. I woke up thinking about you today for some reason, and meant to call you. I guess great minds think alike," said Jimmy.

"I love you Chick," said Jack.

"I love you too, Jackie."

Love is the greatest gift we can give to one another.

Yeah. And I heard that it was always important to be nice to your siblings because parents get old and die. Spouses may get old and die or divorce you. But siblings know you the longest, and generally have the most dirt on you, said Jack with a rueful smile.

Clearly, your brothers love and respect you. It would appear that you have long since been the patriarch of your extended family.

You might say that. Our father made it abundantly clear after our parents split up that it was now his time to really live. Our parents had married young, and dad at age thirty nine decided to live life large. He basically abdicated the throne and put me on it, whether I wanted it or not.

I sense regret on your part.

Regret or anger. They are nearly interchangeable in this regard.

That won't do. Again, Heaven's Code calls for you to forgive all the trespasses against you. It is no different than when someone exhibits passive aggressive behavior in an effort to punish the person who has offended them. The person who is the intended target usually escapes the intended punishment, and it boomerangs on you.

I know. And more often than not, I usually do have the capacity to let it all go, but in moments of high stress, like when you know you are dying, certain old wounds rear their ugly heads, and like stinking rotting decay, permeate the room with their foul odor.

Good word imagery. You must have been dynamite in front of a jury. But seriously, let it go.

I'm trying.

Keep moving if you want some time to play this afternoon. Call your brother.

1225

"Heaven is under our feet as well as over our heads."
—Henry David Thoreau, <u>Walden</u>

"Hey Ju-ju-bee, did I wake you up?" asked Jack.

"Very funny smart aleck. I'm at work," said Jubal Bragg Lee, the youngest son, and named for Generals Jubal Early and Braxton Bragg. It was the consensus of the brothers that he had received the worst name. Their father had been JEB Stuart Lee Jr, and had named all of his boys after Confederate Generals. All were grateful that all had been spared the moniker of Jeb Stuart Lee III. Whenever someone questioned why he would name his sons as he did, and why their mother would allow it as well, he would simply point out that he was a Virginian by birth, and what any critic should be asking is why the United States Army had consistently named so many current active duty posts after these same men from the wrong side of the war! It was a winning argument more often than not.

"Well that's good. It's where you belong today. How's the weather out in Chi-Town?"

"Pretty nice. You should come out and visit. We could go to Wrigley Field and catch the Cubbies. This is their year."

"Spoken like the eternal optimist."

"No really, they are hot this year. Great starting pitching, hitting, fielding. I think this is our year."

"Well I hope so. It would be nice to see it in my life time. Have you caught any games this year?"

"Yeah, but it's expensive to take the whole family, and I hate to be away from them, so more often than not we just watch the games at home."

"Everything is expensive these days," observed Jack.

"Don't I know it! Remember me, I still have a lot of mouths to feed and college tuitions to pay."

"Who told you to keep producing them into your forties? You know there are precautions that one can take to prevent that stuff from happening."

"I wouldn't trade it for the world."

"I know you wouldn't, and that is really good to hear, because it's not like you can take them back to the store."

"I still can't believe that I am having babies and you are a grandfather already," said Jubal.

"And, an empty nester since I was 49," exclaimed Jack.

"Sure, rub it in."

"No, I wouldn't do that. To tell you the truth Juju, there is many a time when I would give anything to go back in time and to have them all around the kitchen table at dinner time again. Heck, most nights, Kathy and I sit at the island in the kitchen, and have dinner with Alex Trebek while we listen to *Jeopardy!* I miss the noise and the bustle of a table full of kids. There is a certain life that the house takes on when there are young people living under the roof."

"I know, I love it. When people ask me where we live I just tell them the corner of Bedlam and Chaos."

"Of course if you don't stop popping them out, pretty soon Shelly will be able buy senior tickets and kid tickets at the movies for you guys, and get a bulk rate on adult and kid diapers for y'all."

"Very funny wise guy."

"You know I'm just giving you a hard time. I think it is great that you and Shelly wanted to have kids of your own…especially at your advanced ages. The trouble with doing that is when they are in high school and dating, you will either not be able to stay awake to wait up for them, or won't be able to hear them sneaking in late in the event your hearing aid batteries go on the fritz. On the bright side, if you do go to bed, you'll be getting up to hit the little boys room every 45 minutes, or be getting up for breakfast to start your day," said Jack with a full head of steam.

"Oh, you are in rare form today my friend."

"Naw. Just keeping you on your toes."

"What's up Colonel? You sound kind of funky," said Jubal.

"Not a thing. Just had some time today, was cleaning out some stuff, and ran across that autographed picture of McLean Stevenson dressed as LTC Henry Blake on *M*A*S*H* that you got for me years ago, and I thought of your ugly face, and thought I would call the resident thespian of the family."

"Wow, you still have that?"

"You know me, sentimental slob that I am, I still have the Popsicle stick box that Becky made for me when she was in second grade sitting out in my study. Of course I still have my Henry Blake picture!"

"That's cool. I'm the same way. Must be something about us September babies that make us think with our hearts."

"Exactly."

"How's the real estate business treating you?"

"Good, no complaints. I am not working nearly as hard as before, and you know, I don't miss it."

"I still can't believe that you gave up being an attorney… without being disbarred or anything. Don't you ever miss it?"

"Naw, I really don't. It had become so dog eat dog that I really don't. Maybe if I had lived one hundred years ago I would still be practicing, but not now."

"You had a gorgeous office, and wow, that power wall behind your desk over the credenza and around the office was pretty impressive. Especially your license from the United States Supreme Court. Pretty cool."

"Didn't mean a thing to me at the end of the day. I was so burned out, and ready for a change, that I couldn't imagine practicing another fifteen, twenty, thirty years. No way."

"But you were good at it," said Jubal.

"Hey, change is good. It keeps us on our toes. How's tricks for you?"

"Knock wood, things are good. I have a couple of exclusive properties downtown that I am responsible for, receivables are up, and the boss is happy. I can't complain, and the hours are a whole lot better since I made the switch."

"See, change is good for you."

"I probably would not have made the change if I hadn't had you as an example of turning your life upside down and inside out. A lot of people thought you were having a mid-life crisis, especially when you started skydiving, race car driving, and wall climbing."

"Hey, no midlife crisis, just a mid-course adjustment."

"Well, whatever you choose to call it, it made a difference in my life too. It seems like you have always been there to blaze the trail for the rest of us."

"I'm the oldest. I have to go first."

"No, that's not it. You were the first Lee in three generations to get a college diploma, much less a masters and a law degree."

"Hey you got a B.A. too...even if it took you seven years," said Jack with a chuckle.

"You had to go there didn't you?"

"Forgive me, but I've been good all day, and you have to admit, for a long time, a lot people were wondering if the movie *Tommy Boy* wasn't a biopic of your life."

"You're a funny man...Not."

"Seriously though, it really wasn't your fault. Nobody was holding you accountable, so why kill yourself?"

"It's still embarrassing. And I did make a point of telling the girls before they left for school that this was definitely a 'do as I say, not as I did' teaching moment."

"Good for you. You know Juju, a lot of what motivated me to get through school as quickly as possible was escaping the dynamic of a rather dysfunctional family life."

"I know. You definitely got the short end of the stick from both Mom and Dad."

"I got over it."

"Did you now?"

"Yeah. I'm where I am at, and I don't owe anybody anything. I did it all by the sweat of my own brow."

"Sometimes I don't think so. Your near maniacal need to over achieve would be a clear indicator that maybe you are still trying to garner daddy's approval and just get mommy to love you in some small way."

"Well Daddy is with the angels, and Mommy, well, that ship sailed a long time ago."

"But it does not make it right, and let's face it, it's not *normal* to have the dysfunctional relationship we all have on and off with our esteemed mother."

"When did you get so smart? Was it those three extra years of college?"

"Uhhhh, no. Actually it was when my doctor told me that most of my stomach issues are a result of this screwy family of ours, and that if I did not come to terms with it, that I would die a very young man, or in the alternative, have a really crappy life because my health would be permanently ruined," Jubal said quietly.

"Makes sense. The important thing Juju is that you made it. You found someone with whom you can share the rest of your life –"

"Third time is the charm."

"Indeed it is. That's what we told you about kindergarten too. And as I was saying, you found someone with whom you can share the rest of your life and enjoy the very essence of why we are here on earth – having families of our own. You are the patriarch of your own clan now dude. You are going to go from just being daddy to granddaddy in a couple of more years when your girls finish college, and watch out, because that's when life gets really interesting."

"I just figured that when I was getting divorced for the second time that everyone was probably thinking that I was just being like dad, and a loser in love."

"No, never anything like that, but we worried about you because of the way you were internalizing the stress in your life and letting your body pay the price."

"I didn't know any other way."

"Just remember Juju, it's not going to be about how many toys you have accumulated. When you stand before the judgment bar and have to account for what you did here on Earth, the questions are going to be along the lines of 'what kind of husband were you? Did you honor your wife? Did you make her life better as a result of being married to you? What kind of father were you? Did you instill the proper life lessons into your children when they were young? Are they productive members of Society today? What kind of legacy did you leave for your posterity?' Those are the questions that you have to have answers to in order to see the other side of Heaven's gate. I am just grateful that I, all of us for that matter, saw the light before it was too late."

"I've always missed our life talks. Do you remember when you came home from Germany on leave? I was only nine years old, hadn't seen you in two years, and Mom wasn't going to let us see one another, and you came and picked me up from school, took me for ice cream, and then dropped me off on the corner where the bus would normally have dropped me?"

"Like it was yesterday kiddo."

"That meant the world to me. I mean I didn't understand why she didn't want me to see my brother, especially when you were the one doing everything right. I mean Jimmy was one step away from jail, and here she was giving you all the static."

"I don't know. I wish I did. But maybe in the next life we'll have all the answers."

"Have you talked to her lately?" asked Jubal.

"Yeah, on her birthday, and Mother's Day. I guess I'll check in with her today as well. Maybe I'll luck out and get her answering machine."

"You're bad."

"Maybe it will be enough to keep me in the will."

"You never know. Well, my secretary is giving me the high sign that I have to get into a meeting. What are you doing now since you clearly are not working? Sounds like you are in the car."

"Very perceptive. You have earned the PGO – phenomenal grasp of the obvious – Award, because I am actually in the car."

"Where you going?"

"Skydiving."

"What? Kathy will kill you."

"Uh, not likely today."

"Why are you going sky diving. I thought you gave that up years ago when you left the Army!"

"You know, there is just something about being free and floating above the ground. The Army has you jump at 1500 feet, even lower when you are in Jump School, I think it was 1200 if my peanut brain does not fail me, and you are down pretty quick. The nice thing about private skydiving, especially when they know that you are retired military, is that they roll out the red carpet for you, and you get to jump at 13,500. You free fall for 8-9000 feet at 120 miles per hour for about 2 minutes, and then you open your chute, and you hang there for another four or five minutes, and you get a totally different perspective of the world. It's like having Heaven above you and Heaven below you all at the same time."

"Well, you do what you want, but no way am I ever going to jump out of a perfectly good airplane much less just for fun."

"Now you sound like the cowardly lion from the Wizard of Oz," said Jack, referencing one of their favorite movies.

"You're talking like the Scarecrow without a brain," retorted Jubal.

"Don't knock it until you try it. It is literally heaven on earth. I understand why the Wright Brothers were so captivated by flight. Your entire perspective really does change."

"Well, have fun, and Geronimo and all that stuff. And I hope for your sake that Kathy does not find out or you'll be a dead man walking unless she finds out because you went splat in some field somewhere, in which case I'll say 'I told you so' when I am standing next to your casket or sponge and zip lock bag assuming it was a big splat. Where are you jumping?"

"Out in Orange County where I used to go years ago."

"Oh yeah. I remember the day that you took me with you and let me watch. That was another cool day and a good memory. Thanks Jackie."

"Love you Jubilee! Be good, and work hard."

"Love you too Jack. Be careful with that chute. Don't get so distracted with Heaven that you forget to pull the ripcord."

"Ciao."

Have you ever read Max Lucado to your children?

Oh yeah. All the time. Beautiful books in messaging and illustration. Why do you ask?

Your reference to your brother about the wizard of Oz made me think of something that Max wrote a while back. "The Wizard [of Oz] says look inside yourself and find self. God says look inside yourself and find [the Holy Spirit]. The first will get you to Kansas. The latter will get you to heaven. Take your pick."

Wow. That's pretty deep.

How do you feel having had the opportunity to __not__ say goodbye to your brothers but to still make them part of your last day?

Better than I thought I would.

Explain.

We all worry about what our legacy is going to be, and I guess from the standpoint of my brothers, I must have done more than okay because they all have good memories of something that I did for each of them. It was like receiving validation for my efforts with them. Sort of like when the kids go off to college and they write, yeah write, or call home to concede that maybe, just maybe, we may have done an okay job of raising them and preparing them for life.

Is that how your brothers made you feel?

Yeah, I think it is.

So this experience so far really has been a gift….

Are you sure that you weren't an attorney in a past life?

Quite sure. I'm in Heaven aren't I?

Oh, and a comedian too!

You seemed pretty eager to dish it out to Jubal a few minutes ago. Can't you take it when it is directed back at you?

I can take it. You just bring it. By the way, what is your name?

What's in a name?

Well, if I am going to spend my last day on Earth with someone, it might be nice to at least have a name to put with the face.

Benjamin.

Benjamin. You know, you look like a Benjamin. That is a strong name.

I've been honored to carry it.

A lot of famous Benjamins in history. Benjamin O. Davis, Senior and Junior. Benjamin Cardozo. Benjamin Butler. Benjamin Spock. Benjamin Harrison. Ben Bradley. Benjamin Netanyahu. Ben E. King. And of course Benjamin Franklin.

You know your Benjamins.

I love history and these were not ordinary men.

We are all ordinary. We can choose to be extraordinary.

Did you choose to be extraordinary Benjamin?

We all chose to be extraordinary when we chose to come to earth and serve our probationary period.

So is this like George Orwell's *Animal Farm* where some animals are more equal than others? Are some spirits more extraordinary than others?

No. It's more the case of the degree to which we embrace and retain Heaven's Code. Again it comes down to choice and agency. You choose the type of life you are going to lead once you make the initial decision to follow the Lord and to attend earth in a probationary status.

I have more questions.

Which we will address later. In the meantime, there is still much for you to do today.

1315

"On earth there is no heaven, but there are pieces of it."
—Jules Renard

"Sorry Colonel, but your certification has long since lapsed. The USPA is pretty clear on what we can and can't do, and unfortunately it has been way too long since you got your initial certification after jump school with the Army."

"I really want to make a jump today. What are my options," asked Jack.

"You can't jump by yourself. There is no way around that without schooling, testing, etc. I can offer you a tandem jump however. It's like wearing a 180 pound back pack that talks," said the ground crewman with an infectious grin.

"I've done that before. Still jumping at 13,500 feet?"

"Yes Sir."

"Okay. Let's do it."

"Would you like to have the experience captured on video?"

"Absolutely," he said, thinking that the kids would get a kick out of it when they watched how he chose to spend his last day.

"Excellent. We'll get you fixed up with Tony on your back and Ernie with a video camera, and you guys can go up in about 40 minutes, assuming that we can get you outfitted and ready to go."

So why do you want to go skydiving today?

It's like that old Tim McGraw song that he wrote for his dad Tug when he was diagnosed with brain cancer. 'I went sky divin', I went rocky mountain climbin', I went 2.7 seconds on a bull name Fu Manchu. And I loved deeper.'

Ah. I get it now. So this is something visceral.

Oh yeah. There is nothing like the view down to the earth. The tranquility of being in the air. Must be what God saw as he created the earth….sorta.

Hmm. Interesting.

Have you ever sky dived before Benjamin?

Actually no. But I do get to experience things vicariously while serving as an escort.

So, today you WILL experience sky diving.

It appears that is correct.

Well hang on to your wings, because this will be a rush for you!

Share with me the 'why' again.

I think skydiving is a way to commune with heaven. It is peaceful and I feel as if I am part of Nature, but nonetheless dependent upon my man-made wings.

Now that is an interesting concept.

It is sort of like the Johnstown Flood.

I fail to see the connection.

Was the flood an act of God or a failure on man's part?

I don't know.

Actually it was both. The rain was the hardest that had ever fallen in the region, but the dam was definitely not up to snuff, and between the missing discharge pipes, the spillway obstructions, and the sag in the center of the dam face, it was the perfect storm. It was *both* an act of God and a failure of man.

Over 2200 souls perished in a matter of minutes.

How do you know that?

How do you know what you know?

Because I read, and acquire knowledge whenever I can.

Exactly. Knowledge is part of Heaven's Code, and is the only thing that you take from this life.

I remember. Benjamin Franklin.

Indeed.

Come on Benjamin, let's go jumping.

"Alright Colonel, you have the altimeter. Make sure you pull the handle when we are at 5,500 feet, and we'll have a nice ride down from there. Do you want to drive this rig?"

"You bet."

"Alright, once we open the chute you can play with the risers and get a feel for it. Just think of me as an oversized back pack. Just steer us towards that open field and put us between the posts on either side of the opening in the fence line. When we go in, we'll do the same sort of landing that you described that you did last time. You slide in on your butt with your legs up in the air, and I'll be on my knees."

"Got it."

"Now, remember to keep your legs up, because if you put them down you're liable to break one or both of your legs, and then I'll break your back. Not good."

"Legs up it is!"

We are doing this why?

It's all about experiencing life Benjamin. You only go around once, well, most of us only go around once.

"On your feet."

"In the door."

"Go, go, go!"

Geronimo.

That's the spirit. No pun intended.

Ohhhhhhhhhhhh.

Hang in there Ben, wait for it, and there.

I didn't like being on my back. I felt like, like a Turtle.

Yes. Like a turtle on its back.

I should have mentioned that part. It only lasts 3 to 4 seconds, but is definitely awkward until you flip over, spread your wings, I mean arms, and are floating on air.

"Watch the altimeter."

"Pulling the cord," and with that there was a rapid ascent that lasted a few seconds until the chute had fully deployed and their leisurely descent to the ground began.

You can see forever up here.

That you can Benny. I told you, a little bit of heaven on earth.

"Legs up, up, up!"

Touch down!

Thank Heaven above.

"Nice landing guys," said Ernie.

"He's a natural," said Tony.

"Thanks."

"You should consider becoming a member and joining the club. Good rates, and we have a lot of fun out here."

"I'll take that under advisement, and if my wife does not divorce me for today, I'll come out again soon."

"Pleasure to have you with us Colonel. Come again."

Was it all that you wanted?

Oh yeah. Definitely the rush that I remember. What did you think?

Well, it certainly was exhilarating.

Benjamin, what is Heaven like?

What do you mean?

I mean is this the last *exhilarating* experience I am going to have because Heaven is all clouds and angels with wings?

As I have told you Jackson, Heaven is delightful. It is all about Light, Love, and Laughter. There are none of the dualities present. The dualities that you experience here on Earth remain here on Earth after serving their purpose as part of your education.

So what is the purpose of Heaven?

The purpose of Heaven is the difference between Eternal Life v. Immortality.

Aren't they one and the same?

Oh no. Anything but.

You say tomato, I say tomatoe.

Oh no, no, no. Far from it.

Immortality is life without death. You can experience that in any number of places. Whereas Eternal Life you get to bask in the glow of God the Eternal Father, where the other righteous souls are, and you can live with your family forever, assuming that they too are worthy.

So death is not the end?

Quite the contrary, it is merely the next step in your life. This earthly existence will be a mere eye blink of your eternal life.

That's quite a bit to absorb in one gulp.

That's why an escort is provided in certain cases.

So I am one of these 'certain cases'? Is that a good thing or a something about which I should be worried?

Jackson, in the absence of duality, there can't be any bad. Remember?

So why are you here then?

If all goes according to the Plan that will become self-evident to you.

When? I don't exactly have a whole lot of time here!

All in due course.

"Charity never faileth."

Yes.

Why did I just say that? I said it didn't I, or did I imagine saying it with my out loud voice?

Indeed you did. And charity suffereth long, and is kind, and envieth not, and is not puffed up, seeketh not her own, is not easily provoked, thinketh no evil, and rejoiceth not in iniquity but rejoiceth in the truth, beareth all things, believeth all things, hopeth all things, endureth all things. Wherefore, my beloved brethren, if ye have not charity, ye are nothing, for charity never faileth. Wherefore, cleave unto charity, which is the greatest of all, for all things must fail.

Okay Benjamin. You are losing me now.

Your life has largely been a life of service and charity to others. The way you took care of your brothers, your own family, your troops in the army, not to mention the relief that you brought a great number of legal clients, some of whom you served on a pro bono basis. Jackson, all of this is charity, and charity never faileth.

Never?

Never. For it is part of Heaven's Code.

1445

> "You'll usually regret the things you do in anger, but
> you'll never regret the things you do in love."
>
> —Unknown.

*The most God-like thing you do in this existence is procreate and bring
new life into it. You create life and then are given a short stewardship before
they leave you to find their own mate and repeat the process.*

You make it sound so noble and regal.

It is.

Do you have a family?

*Yes I do. It is part of the Plan and Heaven's Code. They are a good bit
of the Light that is in my Life.*

Will I have the opportunity to meet them?

If you so desire.

Oh, I certainly would.

Have you gathered your thoughts as to what you want to say to your own children?

I think so.

That is good. Even in today's world, children, even adult children, rely on parents more than ever before, and genuinely need the counsel of their parents.

My kids are pretty independent and self-reliant.

Call them.

"Dr. Lee."

"Hey Bobby, its Dad."

"Well hi Dad. How are you?"

"I'm good. I didn't think you would answer your own phone. Got a minute to talk?"

"Yeah. Liz only works half a day, and I'm just catching up on some patient paperwork. I usually don't pick up the phone, but something told me to pick it up. Strange, huh?"

"How's the head shrinking business these days?"

"Unfortunately for the world, but fortunately for my family, business is booming. There are a lot of nut cases walking around the streets these days," said his son with the same humorous wit that he shared with this father.

"I used to say that if stupidity was a crime that half of my legal clients would be in jail," quipped his father.

"So what are you up to today since I know you don't work an honest forty hour week anymore," teased his son.

"Actually I am driving back from Orange County."

"Oh, Orange County. The only thing I can think of out that way is a certain skydiving business. Did you do something that is going to get you in big trouble with a certain female parent of mine?"

"Ummm, I can neither confirm nor deny such a thing without incriminating myself and making you a co-conspirator," said Jack.

"You are either bored, crying out for attention, or have a death wish," observed his psychologist son.

"Is that your professional opinion?"

"You're a little old for a mid-life crisis, and not nearly as old as George Bush was when he made his first jump at age 80, so yeah, bored, crying out for attention, or a death wish. That would probably sum up the possibilities."

"Well Doctor Freud, as a matter of fact it was just a case of wanting to do something to shake things up and to feel in touch with Nature and Heaven all at the same time."

"My professional advice is not to tell Mom about it, unless you really want to shake things up, because she made it pretty clear at Thanksgiving a couple of years ago that none of the men in her family were even *allowed to think* about skydiving. Something about responsible husbands, fathers, and grandfathers don't engage in such foolhardy activities."

"Are you sure that is what she said," teased his father.

"Uh, yeah! Right before she told me that she would ground me in perpetuity if I allowed you or anyone else to convince me to 'do something as boneheaded as jumping out of airplanes for the sport of it.' For a minute, I feared that she really was going to tattoo it on my arm so that I could look at it if I ever forgot one word of her charge."

"Yes, it's coming back to me now. That *does* sound like your mother."

"So what's up Dad," pressed his son.

"Not a whole lot. I just wanted to call and tell you how proud I am of you, and the life that you have made for yourself with Amy, and to thank you for three great grandkids."

"Well thanks Dad. You sure everything is okay?"

"Absolutely. That is the beauty of skydiving and just hanging out in the clouds; you get a chance to think, put things into perspective and to really prioritize."

"I can see that," said his son quietly.

"Bob, my dad was always too busy doing stuff *for* the family that he never did it *with* us. I never had a game of catch with my Dad. He was never at any of my sporting events, and only eked out enough time to be my Webelos leader when I was ten years old. Otherwise, he was always gone working or doing something around the house. I hope that I didn't do the same thing to you and your sister."

"Dad, you were my best friend growing up. We did everything together. Yeah, you were gone a lot with trials and stuff, and with the Army on the weekends, but when you were home, you were there with us. You were my little league coach, my scout leader for a long time, you came to my games, and when you couldn't, Mom made sure that there was more than enough video tape and pictures to last a lifetime. And you and mom spend a ton of time with our kids, and we are absolutely delighted that you do."

"We always feel like you kids got gypped in the grandparent department. Mom's parents died young, and my folks, well, let's just leave it at that."

"Yeah. Grandma and Grandpa definitely left something to be desired in the grand parenting department. I think the deepest discussion I ever had with Grandpa was about the weather whenever he would call for you and I happened to answer the phone."

"Bob, there's no bigger legacy than our children. Often, they turn out great in spite of our efforts. You made it pretty easy for us. Good athlete, good student, honor society, varsity sports, and you had a good head on your shoulders. We definitely got lucky. I look at some of the guys that I practiced with, or served with, and they did not all get as lucky as your Mom and I did. I watched their struggles and heartache. When your kids struggle, there's nothing worse than that because more often than not it is something beyond our ability to fix."

"I know that Dad. You were a good role model for me, and I am attempting to do the same thing with my kids."

"Stay in touch with them son. Talk to them. I think it is even harder being a parent today than it was when we were raising you and Becky. I always hated it when my clients would call me and need help on behalf of one of their kids. They were willing to spend any amount of money to fix or eliminate the problem, and more often than not the genus of the problem was a lack of communication in their own home."

"I agree. I see it in my practice every day," his son said somberly.

"Too many latch key kids, and so when they start showing signs of problems – with school, or friends, or otherwise — a lot of time it is just too late. Too often I saw problems that had been festering for years that could have been addressed had the parents simply spent more time with their kids," said Jack.

"It's like trying to straighten a tree – it is a whole lot easier to do it as a sapling and to use a couple of ropes and stakes to pull it back to the straight and narrow. At some point it is just too late to straighten that tree," said Robert.

"Exactly right Son."

"I gotta tell ya dad, that watching your own immediate family – Grandma and Grandpa, your brothers – it could have been my dissertation had I wanted to air all the family dirty laundry."

"Why didn't you?"

"For starters, because it would not have been fair to you. Whether you know it or not, you turned out to be an exceptional man. Aside from all of your academic and professional accomplishments, you overcame some pretty big obstacles and built yourself, no, all of us, a pretty remarkable life. You could have perpetuated a bad situation, but chose not do so; instead you chose to create the life that you never had with your own parents. That is pretty amazing Dad, and that is the story I choose to share with patients when they come in here to whine at me about how difficult their lives are and how unfair life has been to them."

"I always believed that living by the Golden Rule would be enough to get me everything that I wanted out of life. I look at your Uncle Jimmy, and I am still awed by the way he managed to turn his life around into something as positive as it is today."

"No thanks to either of your parents. That was all you and Uncle Johnny and Uncle Jubal. You guys stuck together and did what needed to be done, proving that no situation is ever lost. I say to plenty of my family patients that there is always time to improve our relationships with our kids. But, it can't wait another day, especially if it's a relationship that's been neglected for years."

"Amen to that."

"It's all about priorities. You taught me that years ago Pop."

"So Bob, how much of what we are talking about do you attribute to the Society we live in where everyone is plugged in all of the time, but never really communicating?"

73

"What do you mean by that," asked his son.

"Mom and I were out in Seattle last year, had dinner on the Space Needle, and we were watching this family – it could have been ours 20 years ago with a mom, dad, son and daughter – and instead of talking to one another or taking in the sights offered by being 608 feet up in the air, they all had their noses in their respective phones. It took every ounce of self-control and the 'glare' from your mom to keep me in my seat."

"Oh tell me about it. I have a policy that everyone leaves their phone out with Liz or Carrie before coming into my office to talk to me."

"I just worry about the world that your kids, and their kids, are going to inherit from us."

"I hear you Dad."

"It starts with you and me Bobby, and Dan of course," referring to his son-in-law. We're the ones who will ultimately be held accountable for how well or poorly our kids turn out."

"Is this some sort of Harry Chapin *Cats in the Cradle* thing Dad? You okay?" asked his son with an edge of concern in his voice.

"I am just fine, but still feel a little guilty for the things that I missed out on when you and Becky were growing up because I was away for either work or the Army."

"Dad you have nothing to regret. Honestly," implored Robert.

"I don't regret the things that I have done, but I do regret the things I didn't do when I had the chance."

"Like what?"

"Oh, maybe building that balsa wood model of the B-25 Mitchell bomber that you bought for me as a Christmas present one year when you were in high school. You were so proud of finding the same kind of model plane that my dad built back in 1950 when he was 14 years old."

"Hey we were all busy. I was in sports year round, and between your schedules and school, well, you still have the model?"

"As a matter of fact, I do. It is sitting on the shelf in the closet in my study."

"Maybe you and I, or you and Bobby Jr. and I will get around to it one day soon," encouraged his son.

"Remember Bob, kids love their parents, but they love doing stuff with their parents even more. And it doesn't have to be going on a vacation. It can be doing a jigsaw puzzle like I do with Annie whenever I see her, or can be playing catch in the yard, or kicking a soccer ball around like I do with Bobby and Jacob. In my case, I did stuff like learning electrical, or how to panel a room, or to tile a shower, in an effort simply to spend time with my dad. It can be raking leaves, watching a movie, or working on the car. We pass on the essence of who we are, and our kids develop their own strengths, by being together with us, and letting them mirror all of our habits. If we're not making the time to do stuff with our kids, we're throwing away what may very well be a once-in-a-lifetime opportunity. Just remember that your number one priority is to be a good husband and father. After that, its duck soup."

"Good advice Dad. Maybe you should spend some time writing a book or something and impart some of this wisdom."

"Yeah right. The world of parenting by Jackson Lee. We could make it into a movie starring Steve Martin," said Jack.

"I'm serious. I know for a fact that my publisher would welcome a book like that from someone with your background and pedigree," said his son.

"Maybe we could do it together," said Jack, as a lump formed in his throat.

"I'd like that. A lot. Think about it! It could be a lot of fun capturing the myriad of stories that you have shared with us over the years. There might even be a salient point or two that someone else might learn something from and put into practice," he added with a chuckle.

"You're a good man Bobby Lee," said Jack.

"I learned from the best Pop," said his son.

"My love to Amy and the kids."

"I love you too Dad."

That was powerful.

He's a great man.

He had a pretty significant model to emulate.

He's going to run circles around me every which way.

Don't sell yourself short. The fruit doesn't have a habit of falling too far from the tree.

That's kind of you to say Benjamin, but both Bobby and Becky were pretty exceptional kids, and knock wood, found their soul mates and have started their own families.

It's because you and Kathy followed Heaven's Code. You brought light, and love and laughter into the home that you built so many years ago.

Is it wrong for me to say that despite all that I am hearing and seeing today that I still don't want to go?

Not wrong, and definitely a very human emotion.

1515

> "A daughter may outgrow your lap, but she
> will never outgrow your heart."
>
> —Unknown.

"Hi honey, it's Dad."

"Oh am I glad you called," exclaimed Rebecca Lee Curtis. "I really need your help on this one Daddy."

"Sounds serious," teased Jack.

"Don't you know it," said Becky, not picking up on her father's facetious tone.

"Your granddaughter asked me a question today and I don't know how to answer it. Every time I think about how to frame up my answer, I start to cry."

"Oh, I'm sorry honey. Lay it on me."

"She wanted to know, 'do people look the same when they go to heaven, mommy?' I was so taken aback by the question that I just stood there speechless."

"Wow. That is definitely a tough one, especially from a four year old."

"Have you given her any type of an answer?"

"Well yeah. I said 'I don't know. I don't think so,' and then realized that it was a lame answer and told her that I would get back to her."

"And did you?"

"Apparently not quickly enough, because she asked me about it again at lunchtime, and I told her that I wasn't sure."

"What happened then," asked Jack, slipping back into his trial attorney persona.

"She screwed up her face as if to say 'are you stupid mommy' and then said, 'then how do people recognize each other?' Why would a four year old ask such questions," asked his daughter.

I hope it is not because she knows that her grandfather is going to die, thought Jack, as a lump came to his throat.

"Have you asked Dan if he has any brilliant insights into how to answer this question?"

"Oh I did. I most certainly did. And his brilliant suggestion was for me to call you!"

"I must say, 'then how do people recognize each other?' is certainly cutting to the chase."

"She is definitely your granddaughter."

"Brilliance does run in the family, but I've heard that it often skips a generation," quipped Jack.

"That must be true, because Grandpa JEB once told me the same thing," she said without skipping a beat.

"Touché, my dear. Touché."

"I was literally picking up my phone to call you when you called me, because she asked me a *third* time when she got up from her nap."

"What did you tell her?"

"I said, 'I don't know, sweetie. Everyone has a perfect body and because our hearts are connected, we just feel it when we meet someone from our own family. That you might meet great-grandma Lee when she was a little girl your age, but you would know her because your heart will tell you who she is and that you are part of the same family. It's all about the heart.' Pretty dumb huh?"

"Not at all. In fact that is a pretty great answer all things considered. Did she buy it?"

"I think so, but she is so blasted smart that I never know what is going on in that head of hers."

Jack. Share with her what you read in the scriptures during your personal study last week. It will be helpful.

"Dad, you there?"

"Oh yeah. I was just thinking about something that I read last week during my own personal scripture study. I'm just trying to recall exactly how it was phrased."

"Please, I am all ears because I need your help."

"It was along the lines of, 'The implication of Scripture is that we will know our loved ones in heaven both before and after resurrection.'"

"Right."

"The disciples were able to recognize the Lord after His death and resurrection, though sometimes when he desired to remain incognito, they did not recognize Him, especially when he disguised himself. Normally, however, they were able to recognize Him. Scripture teaches us that we will have a glorified body like his which suggests that what was true of His body will be true of ours. So, the only real question is what will we look like? Will I be the same age you are now when we meet in Heaven, or will we both be children? Will we be the age at which we die? I don't know. But somehow, somehow, we will know that I am your father and that you are my daughter."

"Oh daddy."

"So, if Jesus was resurrected, with a perfect body, we will be as well. I am taking a leap of faith when I say that we will be able to recognize our loved ones in heaven. I think your explanation was absolutely perfect sweetheart," said Jack.

"But there has to be more to it than that," started Becky.

"Oh there is. But for a four year old, that is probably good enough. Heck it is probably good enough for a fifty seven year old."

"Well I understand that the Bible says that when we die that we can either have eternal life or eternal death," she began.

"Yes. But think of it rather as either eternal life or immortality."

"What's the difference?"

"Funny you should ask that. I asked the very same thing to a friend of mine who was explaining the difference to me when I didn't get it."

"Pray continue professor, I am all ears," said his daughter.

"Those who place their faith in Jesus Christ receive everlasting life. We want to live forever in the presence of God the Eternal Father."

"Right. I'm with you so far."

"When a believer dies, her body remains in the grave. It is a mere shell; it was a vehicle by which she was able to accomplish her earthly mission. In the meantime, her spirit is consciously and immediately taken into the presence of Jesus."

"So when we die, we go to Heaven."

"If you believe, yes."

"And you know this how?"

"How do we know anything? It's all faith. Faith in things unseen. It's a feeling. And this just feels right to me."

"So what is immortality?"

"Oh, right. Immortality is just that – living forever. Eternal life on the other hand is living in the presence of God. Where there is light, laughter, and love." *Where did that come from,* mused Jack.

"Oh daddy. Do you really believe that when we die our soul's immediate destiny is heaven?"

"If I was to play attorney, I could say that since Jesus himself ascended into heaven and is presently there preparing dwelling places for us in which to live, that it is a pretty good bet that this is how it is going to play out."

"How neat would that be to know that was what was going to happen to each of us," mused his daughter.

"You can know it, if you have faith," said her father, listening to himself as the words left his lips.

"I do, I do," she said, sounding very much like the little girl with whom he used to have secret breakfasts while her mother and brother often slept in on Sunday mornings.

"So besides deep theological questions keeping you on your toes, what else is going on with you?"

"Oh my gosh Dad. The days fly by. Once the school day ends, between homework, gymnastics, girl scouts, soccer, and just keeping up with everything around the house, my life is an absolute blur. Mom made it look so easy that I now I know that she must have supernatural powers. I wish I had inherited them from her," exclaimed his daughter.

"From where I am seated, you are doing a pretty spectacular job raising three kids under eight years of age," said her father proudly.

"They grow up so fast, you know?"

"Oh yeah I do. My baby girl is raising three of her own babies now," he said with a soft chuckle.

"Does it ever get easier?"

"Uh, no. Well, there is a short time in their life where they will think they know more than you, and ignore you completely, but then something happens, they realize that you are not half as stupid as you look, and they come back to the fold, asking questions, and actually become quite personable," observed her father.

"Oh daddy. Bobby and I weren't that bad as teenagers."

"No you weren't... as teenagers go. Not like some of your cousins certainly. But you each went through a period where you explored, pushed us away ever so slightly, and had to find yourselves," he recalled wistfully. "And I would not have had it any other way. Everyone needs this time to sort things through and discover their inner self."

"Wow. When did you become so wise Solomon?"

"I don't know. It sort of just catches up with you. I think it starts with realizing that contrary to what we want to believe, we *don't* have all the answers, are not the be all, end all hot stuff, and that we have to acknowledge that there are forces larger than ourselves at work in the universe."

"When did you figure out that gem of wisdom," asked his daughter obviously intrigued by the thought.

"About ten years ago. It was also when I realized that 95% of what I used to worry about, sometimes tying myself up in knots about, never came to fruition and that it was nothing more than a waste of time and energy to worry about things over which I had no control."

"What happened when you had this realization?"

"Life became far more bearable, it became easier to accept, and I had a greater vision of the direction I wanted to take my life. Hence the career change, and the re-ordering of my priorities."

"That must have made you feel pretty good too," she said softly.

"It did. For all the years that I lived at warp speed, heaping pressure on myself to achieve and to always be on top of everything, it also proved to be quite liberating."

"You never forced your ideas of hyper-achievement on to Bobby and me," began his daughter.

"No, I tried not to do that, but I did want you to magnify your talents, and to maximize your potential, which you both did admirably," said her father.

"It helped that we had parents who were supportive, and loved us without reservation."

"Is that how you really felt? Loved and supported?"

"Dad, when we were kids there was never a doubt that we were loved, well cared for, and that we were part of the Lee team. A lot of our friends didn't come close to having what we had, and I don't mean money and all that stuff."

"What was the best part of your childhood," asked her father.

"The fact that we knew beyond any doubt that you and mom loved one another and also the two of us. So many of our friends grew up not even secure in that knowledge. Several of our friends wanted to be adopted by you and mom so that they could be part of our family. That alone kept us from taking what we had for granted. Every time one of our friends had their lives blow up when one of their parents decided that it was time to leave the family for one reason or another, it made us appreciate the stability that you and mom offered us all the more."

"I don't want to burst your bubble kitten, but it was not all wine and roses and always smooth sailing for your mom and I as a couple; we had our rough spots, usually attributable to my schedule and frankly, my upbringing. Your mom brought out feelings in me that I never knew I had, and really helped me grow as a person well beyond just expanding my horizons in terms of foods that I eat," he said with a softness that had crept into his voice.

"We never knew if you and mom weren't getting along."

"We made sure that you didn't. Unlike you, my childhood memories of my parents are filled with *years* of sound-bites that spoke of divorce, dissatisfaction, and deception."

"That must have been awful," said his daughter.

"I didn't realize how awful it was until I was an adult, and then became a father in my own right."

"How does one simply decide to be different," asked Becky. "How did you do it?"

"If it hurts enough, it becomes easy to embrace the desired change. Benjamin Franklin used to carry a card with him that contained that quarter's desired wish list of thirteen habits he wanted to make or break, things he wanted to implement, or ways that he wanted to improve himself. At the end of thirteen weeks he would then change things up and develop a new list. I never did it as formally as all that, but I would make resolutions about how I was going to conduct myself."

"For example," she asked.

"For example, when your mom and I first got married, we had to learn to live with one another. As you well know, even if you love someone, you still have to adapt from living as one person to living as part of a couple. There needs to be compromise and communication. Well, mom's parents like to communicate *loudly* from time to time, especially when they are debating the merits of a particular subject on which they might not agree."

"Oh yeah, I can recall many a time when Grandma and Grandpa would discuss things loudly, but they always resolved their issues."

"That they did, and that is why they are still married some fifty odd years later."

"So that's healthy then right?"

"Apparently it works for them. As for me and mom, well, because I saw what arguing did to my parents, and how my mother would often say things in anger to either my dad or to me or one of my brothers, I resolved that I would *never* say anything in anger that I would want to take back and obviously not be able to do so."

"So…"

"So, the first time mom and I disagreed on something, she was ready to drop the gloves and go at it for fifteen rounds, and I just didn't. I couldn't. To this day, the angrier I get, the quieter I get. Because I never want to hurt anyone that I love or care about with words that sting. So, I don't say anything. At least until I have mastered my emotions and can trust my voice. That's hard to take if you have some Irish blood in you like your mom does."

"So you and mom never argued?"

"Far from it. We just learned how to argue fairly and honestly, and not to denigrate our marriage and our family by being mean or dirty. Truth be told, and I am not proud of this by any stretch, but your father was the king of passive-aggressive behavior. Your brother would probably have a field day with me on his couch," said Jack with a rueful chuckle.

"So what makes you and mom such a great couple?"

"You writing a book or something?" quipped Jack.

"No, no. no. It's just that Dan and I were talking the other night about our marriage, our friends, our parents, our siblings, and we agreed that you and mom are probably one of the best couples we know, and want to be like you." said his daughter with a slight catch in her voice.

"Well for starters, if you were *talking* about your marriage, you are probably light years ahead of your peers. Make no mistake about it, marriage is hard work. It is probably the hardest thing you will do in life. It requires constant nourishment and reinforcement. There are so many negative forces out there attempting to tear marriages apart. We live in a disposable world, where everything, to include relationships can be replaced in the blink of an eye. There are temptations, and societal acceptances of things now that were just not done twenty, thirty, forty years ago. I suspect that your grandparents are still married because divorce was just that foreign a concept to their generation."

"You may be right about that, when I stop to think about it."

"There was one summer when I was practicing law that I handled three divorce cases for couples who were fairly old, yikes, they were the age that I am now. All mid 50's in age, all three had been married 36 years – how's that for coincidence – and all were splitting up because they had 'grown apart,' 'didn't see eye to eye any more', or 'simply wanted a change in their lives.' All three cases were extremely amicable, the kids were all grown – because all of them had stayed together for the sake of the kids, they largely agreed on how to split pensions and property, and I was left to believe that I was the only one grieving for each of their marriages. I hated it, hated doing that type of law, and felt dirty afterwards. That was another reason I did more regular trial work where there were defined winners and losers. I determined then and there that there is no such thing as a good divorce and that the only winners were the attorneys of record."

"Did it make you appreciate your marriage more," asked his daughter.

"Oh you know it. It made me appreciate your mom more, the two of you, and given my family's checkered background, you all became my refuge from the world."

"So it was something that you became conscious of, and did not take for granted," said Becky.

"Exactly. It drove me to be a better husband and father, and probably served as the impetus for my eventual career change. I just knew what I wanted out of life. But like I said, marriage is hard work, and if both parties are not committed, you can't do it by yourself. It requires two to make it, and two to break it."

"But anything worth having usually does require work and sacrifice."

"Right again pretty girl. That's why good marriages may be hard to achieve, but when they are achieved, are so much sweeter a victory. Being a parent is easy by comparison, because the bond between parent and child is forever. You can't divorce your kids, well, unless you are my mother, but you know what I mean."

"Unqualified love and acceptance."

"Exactly."

"So what's the secret to a successful family?"

"Making time for you and Dan as a couple, as individuals, as well as spending as much time with the kids individually one on one, and collectively as a family. I had an old friend that I used to work with who used to tell me, 'when it comes to parenting, it's not just *quality of time* that's important, it's *quantity of time*.' I remember falling into one of the traps that he warned me about when I was first starting out as an attorney. When- ever I would get so busy at work that I couldn't make it home for dinner or for bedtime, or I was traveling, I would comfort myself while staying late at the office again with the idea that I would make it up by taking you and Bobby to a ballgame or the zoo or to a movie over the weekend. As long as I spent some quality time with you guys, or mom, I would think, it will all balance out. It probably didn't."

"It worked for your friend right," asked Becky.

"Uh no. He ended up divorced, married to two other people before finally getting it right, and had rocky relationships with his kids until he finally established his priorities, and started practicing what he preached. He and a later wife had kids of their own, and the way he interacts with them is a far cry from how he related to his older kids. In some ways I am happy for him, but sad for him at the same time. By the same token, I know lots of busy guys who take control of their schedules in order to either be at home for dinners more or be at those special school events with the kids. Kids do remember that."

"I remember you coming to events straight from court with your suit on still, or from the army still wearing your uniform," she said.

"Learning from other's mistakes is a whole lot less painful than learning them from your own."

"Wow, another very profound observation. Two in the same day," she quipped.

"Obviously I failed as a father in keeping you from developing a rather sarcastic wit. Where did you ever develop such a habit?"

"Gee, I don't know. I guess the fruit didn't fall far from the tree," she said.

"Remind me, and I'll slap your mother later for that nasty habit."

"Yeah right. It was all mom on that score," she said with a laugh.

"Your mom and I just wanted you and Bobby to be happy, healthy, and well adjusted. Your mom used to say that she didn't want either of you to excel at any one thing that would make you superior to everyone else, like being an Olympic gymnast or a Rhodes Scholar – because the *sacrifice* that these people endure often makes life very difficult for them to live as ordinary people."

"So average is good," she said.

"So long as average means that you have your feet firmly planted on the ground while you stretch and reach for the stars in terms of maximizing your talents."

"You make it sound simple."

"It's anything but simple."

"So what is the secret to life Daddy?"

"Well, at least we know where Annie gets the deep questions," he began.

"Is there a secret to a happy life," she pressed.

"I think it is all about light, laughter, and love," he began, again questioning the passion that he was feeling as he uttered the words.

"Light, laughter, and love. That's it?"

"Isn't that enough?"

"I can't imagine a more perfect world if it were full of nothing but light, laughter, and love," she said as her heart swelled accompanied by the witness that her father had never spoken truer words.

"Things are not going to get easier for your kids or your grandkids. Your job is to be an umbrella that keeps the worst of the world off of your family, and to just make your piece of the vineyard a better place by being a good example to your family, your friends, and by serving as a beacon of light."

"I think you are doing that right now daddy," she said as she stifled a tear.

"It took me a lot of years to figure all this out. I just want better for you and Bobby and all of the grandkids. The world is getting scarier and scarier every day, and I had always hoped to be around for a long

long time to be there as the white knight who can still wield the sword of truth and justice on behalf of the underdog and the downtrodden, but you never know when life may throw you a curve ball. That's why you have to live each and every day to the fullest, dance like nobody is watching, and never allow your priorities to become muddled like I did years ago."

"I love you Dad."

"I love you too sweetie. You have always been my treasure, and a great source of light, laughter, and love in my life. You are a great mom, and Dan is very lucky to have you as his wife. You've been a pretty good daughter too."

"Do you remember when you were in graduate school and I had afternoon kindergarten, and we were home together in the morning?"

"I sure do. Mid-morning snacks, while we watched *Love Boat* reruns, and then I would go back to working on my thesis."

"Those days are some of my favorite memories," she said with a sob.

"Why is that?"

"Because it was just you and me. You were busy working on your thesis, but as soon as 10 o'clock rolled around, and Sesame Street was over, I knew that for the next hour you were all mine. You would play with me, or we would have a tea party, or you would read to me. It was a magical time."

"I'm glad that you have those memories, especially when I pulled my disappearing act after becoming a trial lawyer," he said quietly, not trusting is voice.

"I know that Bobby has the same type of memories of when you were in scouting together and would go camping and share a tent, cook salmon on a cedar plank while all the other guys were dining on beans and wienies, or cooking eggs in orange rinds and onion skins in the camp fire, and best of all baking cookies over coals in your famous cardboard box easy bake oven."

"Really?"

"Oh yeah. In fact last month he and Amy were over here with the kids for a barbeque and after we had grilled brats and burgers, he took the coals out of the grill and made an easy bake oven out of a file box, and baked cookies for all the kids out on the patio. You should appreciate the fact that he gave full attribution for the concept to their grandfather, so the kids think you are genius in your own time."

"Wow. That's really neat."

"Dad, you gave us a good life, and a good start on how to raise our own kids. Don't ever doubt your efforts. We know that you weren't perfect, but neither one of us would have traded any aspect of our childhood with any of our friends."

"Thanks sweetie."

"Well I have to go pick up Jamie at a friend's house, so bring mom over for dinner on Sunday. We'll throw something on the grill and you can bake cookies for all of us."

"Sounds like a date, and I'll bring a suitable box if you make up the cookie dough," he said, knowing that it was not to be…

"Love you Daddy."

"I love you too sweetheart."

1545

"Seeing death as the end of life is like seeing
the horizon as the end of the ocean."

—David Searls

How are you feeling at this moment?
Drained.
*I can appreciate that; many of the spirits that I have escorted who have
had this opportunity have expressed it much the same way.*
How did you feel, assuming that you had the same opportunity?
I did, and it was a mixed blessing.
How so a mixed blessing?
*My son was graduating medical school, and I was so looking forward to
calling him doctor, and referring to him as 'my son the doctor,' but it was
not to be – I died the month before his commencement exercise.*
How did you die?

Do the gates of Heaven swing in or swing out?

I beg your pardon.

Does it really matter?

I mean was it sudden, or did you have an accident?

It was relatively sudden. I had an aortic aneurism that had never been diagnosed. When it ruptured, I was gone almost immediately. Had its existence been known, a cardiac surgeon could have repaired it.

That's how most people profess to wanting to die – there one minute, gone the next.

That may be true, but a slow death allows one to prepare. Dying as I did is no less a shock when it happens and one finds themselves progressing towards Heaven; imagine if you did not have today to help you prepare for your transition?

I see your point. What will it be like?

Much as you discussed with your daughter, you will have a perfect body and enjoy the Lord's rest.

What does that mean – the Lord's rest?

His glorious presence for eternity.

Are you with me the entire time?

I will be with you until you are through the gates of Heaven and are met by the Savior himself.

Oh really? How does that work. I always thought St. Peter manned the gates, and had the clipboard to determine who gets in and who does not.

The Savior himself serves as the gatekeeper of the celestial kingdom not to exclude people, but to personally welcome and embrace those who have made it back home.

Oh my.

What is it?

I, I just had a tremendous feeling in my heart that what you just explained is the absolute truth. Until today I had never really considered that dying could be just another step in a progression, and that it would be like going home.

Comforting isn't it?

Very much so, though to be honest, I still harbor feelings that I don't want to go home quite yet.

Why is that do you think?

It may be because I just plunked down $50 for a five year warranty on a new watch battery —-

Jackson.

But really because I still have unfinished work here with my family. At least I would like to think that is the reason, but then again, it just may be that I am still human enough that I want to leave on my own terms, and merely want more time with my family.

It's not about our timetable, but rather that of Heaven.

I suspected that you would say something like that; are you sure that you were not an attorney in a past life?

Quite. I was actually a teacher.

Oh really. What did you teach?

I taught high school science where there were hard and fast rules of Nature with ancillary theorems that kept a certain order to things.

I can see you teaching science Benjamin.

Why is that?

Your personality lends itself to the rules of science.

I also believe that practicing Obedience is another higher form of science.

With rules and reactions that govern us accordingly.

Exactly.

I feel as if you continue to open my eyes to principles that I may have had laying around in my subconscious but have never truly addressed.

Regardless of a person's chosen faith, at the end of their life's journey, they stand before the judgment bar. As you shared with your family earlier, it is not about the number of toys or wealth accumulated that determines your eligibility or qualification for entrance into the Lord's rest. Rather, it is about measuring your heart.

Measuring my heart? How?

As you are aware, all that you will take with you is your knowledge and your character, which in turn will be measured in two ways. One, the weight of your conscience – a record of your life in terms of good deeds and bad deeds — will be examined. If found wanting, you won't advance. If the weight of the good deeds exceed those of the bad ones — this is as much an assessment of your ethics and integrity — did you live the golden rule and treat others as you would want to be treated — the impurities of your heart will be removed and as if equipped with the feathers of a bird's wings, your soul will give flight. The purer your heart, the lighter your spirit will be, and the higher you will ascend. Like Icarus who desired to fly, you will seek out the sun in the sky but without fear of the sun melting the wax that attaches your wings. You will go towards the light, the laughter, and love of Heaven.

And the second way?

As a corollary to the first weights and measures test, it will also be a test of your faith and testimony. Are you a true believer? Was there true congruence between your words and actions here on earth?

That is an interesting choice of words and the use of congruence, especially for a scientist.

It is actually a very appropriate term. But to put it in other terms that you may find more readily acceptable: did you walk the walk while talking the talk?

That I can understand Benjamin.

Well?

Well what?

Have you lived your life in congruence with the tenets of your faith?

I think so. I want to think so. I certainly hope so. I hope that I will be judged worthy of advancement. I can't imagine that you are here but for the fact that someone up there believes that I am worthy of an escort such as yourself because I will be deemed appropriate for advancement. Would I be too far off the mark to believe that you are here for that reason?

I am not certain if I am in the presence of an attorney or a scientist. The logic of your argument is nearly irrefutable.

But something tells me that it is not as simple as my theory would purport it to be. It is not that simple is it Benjamin?

Why would you say that?

Me thinks that if it were that simple, that I would not be going through the exercise that we are going through. We would simply be on our way to the gates of Heaven. There is a reason that I am playing the part of Ebenezer Scrooge and you get the co-starring role of the Ghost of Christmas Past.

All things pertaining to Heaven are on the Lord's timetable. It is not ours to question.

Now you sound like a loyal politician quoting the party line.

Remember Jackson, it is all on the Lord's timetable and what is in your heart that will determine the outcome of today.

Are you saying that the outcome of today has *not* already been foreordained?

I will repeat for your edification that today is a great gift that you have been afforded because of the exemplary life that you have lived while in your probationary status.

So I should shut up and go with the flow.

I could not have said it any better or any plainer.

1640

"It's like doughnut holes. Whether you take a doughnut hole as a blank space or as an entity unto itself is a purely metaphysical question and does not affect the taste of the doughnut one bit."

—Haruki Murakami

Remember what we said about regrets. They weigh down your heart. You should not knowingly go before the Judgment Bar with any unnecessary regrets.

So what you are saying is that I should call my mother.

I am saying that you have your agency, and can do as you please, but it may be to your advantage to call her and to resolve any issues that may transform into regrets that only serve to weigh down your heart. Clearly it is too late to talk to your father; that will have to wait until you see him on the other side.

He's there?

Of course he's there. You are surprised?

Well, based on what you have shared with me, I was a little curious at just where the bar is set and where the cut offs are for the varying degrees of glory of which you have spoken.

Jackson, Father is loving, and forgiving, and very accepting. Think about your own children when they have done things that were not pleasing to you and Kathy. You didn't cast them out, or cease to love them. Imagine the sheer amount of disappointment that our Heavenly parents have experienced with all of their children.

Yikes, I never thought of it quite that way before.

Call your mother; for her sake, and yours.

I couldn't just have two root canals without anesthetic and simply call it even?

Regrets, Jack. Regrets. We want your heart as light as a feather.

"Hello."

"Hi Mom, its Jack."

"Oh hello," she said in that tone of voice that conveys that he is an intrusion.

"How are you?"

"Well my arthritis is bothering me, and I have had a terrible stomach on and off for a week now. I actually had to re-schedule my hair appointment because I was afraid that I wouldn't be able to sit still long enough for her to wash and set my hair."

"I'm sorry to hear that."

"I even stayed home from the nickel slots tournament that I was going to participate in because I just was not up to it. I have so many points at the casino that I actually got Jimmy a room for free when he came out to visit. They love me there. They can't do enough for me. They are always comping me for meals and drinks."

"Uh huh."

"And all of my wonderful "adopted-daughters" have been so attentive. They bring in meals for me, continue to do all of my shopping and continue to drive me everywhere I need to go. I am so glad that I got rid of the car when Reubie died. I simply don't need it."

"Why do you have them do all that for you when you are perfectly healthy *and able* to get around yourself?"

"They want to do it, and I don't like driving."

"Why don't you have them drive you to the store and you do your own shopping?"

"They tell me not to worry about it."

"Are you walking to the club house and around the neighborhood?"

"Not so much anymore. I just don't like walking anymore."

"It will keep you both young and alive," he advised.

"Oh they think I am fifty five at the casino."

"Really," he said, all the while wondering how many were in need of an eye exam.

"Oh yeah. Your mother still has quite a figure."

"Uh huh."

"So?" she asked, implying it was his turn to say something about himself.

"Work is good, kids are great, and we are having a ball with the grandkids. I think we are going to take them to Disney World soon."

"Uh huh. Did I tell you that I bought a new television for the living room?"

"No. How come?"

"One of the girls thought I could use a bigger one so that I could see it easier from the kitchen table."

"What did you do with the old one? Move it into your bedroom?"

"No, I gave it to Alexis."

"Who?"

"One of my girls."

"So, what had you been doing before you got sick," he asked, grasping at straws as he usually did during these unilateral discussions.

"Oh, just watching television. Sometimes I will go to dinner with one of the girls when they take me shopping or something."

"Watched any good movies lately?"

"Only if they are on regular television. I gave up the extra channels we had because the only ones that I really need are QVC and HSN. I have twelve new purses, and they are all beautiful leather."

"What do you need twelve additional purses for if you don't go out?"

"Oh I don't know. I gave a lot of the old ones away to the girls because they are so good to me, so I had the space for the new ones in the closet anyway. I do go out to the casino three times a week. The purses are so much easier to keep my nickels in than in those big popcorn cups that they provide."

"Uh huh."

"Have you talked to your brothers lately?"

"As a matter of fact I talked to all three of them today."

"Really? Why?"

"Why? Because they are my brothers, we love one another, and because I have the time now that I am not working seventy hours a week."

"What did you talk about?"

"You know, every conversation was totally different. We talked about our wives, kids, work, vacations, grandkids, you know, the stuff family members talk about when they call one another."

"Did you talk about me?" she asked.

"Actually Mom, not so much. We have so much going on in our own lives with our kids and grandkids that the time flies by, especially if the boys are at work, then we can't gab forever like we sometimes do on the weekends."

"What do you talk about then?"

"Oh I don't know. It could be sports, vacations, retirement plans, or work, or back to the family. I talked to Johnny the other day for almost two hours while I was walking all the trails in my neighborhood. The time just flies by sometimes, especially when we talk about stuff that we did when we were kids," he said.

"What else?"

"Sometimes we have serious discussions about something one or both of us have read or heard about on the news."

"Like what?"

"Oh I don't know. Presidential politics, the state of the world, terrorism, or something personal."

"About me?"

"No."

"Then what?" she said, her voice becoming a bit shriller than usual.

"Mom, do you believe in Heaven?"

"Why would you ask me that? Do you want me to die?"

"No, of course not. But if we are thinking about it in our fifties, surely you think about stuff like that in your seventies don't you?"

"Not really."

"Don't you want to see your parents again?"

"Of course. But you don't have to dwell on things like that while you are alive."

"Mom, you are seventy eight years old now. You've lived a long time. Don't you have any regrets for things you have done, or said, or didn't say or didn't do at some point in your life?"

"Why would you ask me something like that?"

"You asked me what the boys and I talk about. Sometimes we have discussions on topics such as these. With the exception of Jubal, we are all grandfathers now, and our grandkids ask some pretty tough questions. Just today Annie asked how she would recognize members of our family in heaven."

"Who's Annie?"

"Your great-granddaughter, Becky's little girl."

"Oh. How old is she now?"

"Four. Going on fifteen sometimes. She is gorgeous and smart as a whip. So what do you think?"

"About what?"

"Annie's question."

"I don't know. I've never thought about it. Why would a four year old be thinking about something as morbid as that?"

"I don't think it is morbid. I think it is perfectly natural for kids to be curious about things, and with the internet and movies, kids are much more aware of things around them than when we were kids and all we had to worry about was whether there was air in our bicycle tires and whether we had fifteen cents for a Good Humor bar."

"I don't like the internet, and that's why I got rid of the computer when Reubie died too. I just didn't have a need for it."

"What did you do with it? Did you take off all of your personal data on it? I know that Reuben kept all of your financial stuff on it," said Jack.

"I gave it to one of my adopted daughters. There wasn't anything to take off of it, because the slot thing was empty."

"Mom, I'm talking about taking *data* off of it. That was very personal information that nobody needs to know about."

"I don't know what you are talking about."

"Mom, your personal financial information was on there. It needs to come off."

"I'm not worried about it."

"Okay, it's your business. You could have given it to one of your own grandkids you know."

"Why would I do that? They never call me."

"Do you ever call them?"

"They should call me. I am the grandmother. You know, you and your brothers could call me more too. And I never hear from Kathy anymore. We used to be closer than most mothers and daughters."

"She's teaching full time again Mom. She leaves at seven o'clock in the morning, and if she isn't involved in coaching, she still does not get home much before five thirty or six o'clock. A lot of times I do the cooking now because I am home before she is."

"You're cooking? If she's working that many hours then you should be taking her out for dinner."

"Sometimes we do go out. But more often than not, she just wants to come home, slip off her shoes, have a glass of lemonade, talk to me over dinner, and then she usually has home work papers to grade or lesson plans to review or put together. Sometimes we go over to Bobby's or Becky's or they'll pop over with the kids."

"Oh."

"It's awesome living near the kids and seeing the grandkids on a regular basis."

"Uh huh."

"You know Mom, I heard John Maxwell speak down in Atlanta and he said that 'your grandkids are your reward for not killing your own kids.'"

"Who's John Maxwell?"

"He is one of my favorite authors on leadership."

"Why would he say that about killing his own kids?"

"He was making the point that grandchildren are the pot of gold at the end of the rainbow after you have toiled to raise and support your own kids."

"Oh. I guess that makes sense. Raising kids is hard."

"I know. I guess that is why you used to lock me and Johnny out of the house after lunch during our summer break when we lived out in Roanoke."

"I never locked you out."

"Sure you did. You'd take a nap, and a lot of times we would jiggle open the sliding glass door on the patio so that we could get in and use the bathroom or grab the Fudgsicles that we used to lick and hide in the back of the freezer in the storage room," said Jack.

Why do you say things like that? I never locked you out of the house. Do you tell people lies about me like that?"

"No Mom. I never lie."

"Then you should not make up stories like that. They are not nice."

"Mom, do you ever miss your parents?" he asked, changing the subject.

"Of course."

"Do you think you will see them again?"

"Yes."

"Do you ever think about calling Aunt Evelyn?"

"No. Never."

"But Mom, she's your sister. Your own sibling. It's been what, twenty five *years* since you have spoken to her?"

"I don't want to talk to her or any member of her family."

"You know Mom, life is short. You're seventy eight, and she's seventy six. You guys aren't getting any younger."

"There you go again, putting me in an early grave," she shrieked.

"Nobody is putting you into an early grave Mom. We just want peace in the family. Everyone knows what is going on in the family courtesy of Facebook except you. It's as if you are a hermit out there in Vegas."

"I'm just fine with my family out here."

"Mom, they aren't your family. They are nice people who are either taking pity on a senior citizen or vultures positioning themselves to prey on you like that stupid financial advisor that I warned you about."

"She was horrible, but was she was nice at first."

"Well of course she was nice at first, that's how she was luring you in. And while financial advisors can be trustees, they are never beneficiaries. My gosh Mom, she was a freaking crook."

"I'm not calling Evelyn. She's dead to me."

"Okay, have it your way. I'm just telling you that I love having three brothers, and lots of nieces and nephews that send me messages, and include me as part of their lives, and that are part of one another's lives as they interact with their cousins."

"I don't want Evelyn or any of her family in my life," the venom obvious in the tone of her voice.

"Well what about your own grandkids and great grandkids? You used to say that you couldn't or wouldn't travel because of Reuben. He's gone now, so what's your excuse for not coming to visit us?"

"You don't come to visit me," she responded in kind.

"Mom, we all work, and have lives with kids and activities. You could come here and we could entertain you, and share you, but it's as if you want no part of us either. That's not normal."

"Don't you go telling me what is normal and what is not," snapped his mother.

"Mom, I didn't call you to upset you. I'm sorry that you are not feeling well right now, but when you are feeling better, you should seriously think about jumping on a plane and visiting all the boys and re-connecting with your own family. There is going to come a time when you won't be healthy enough to do this, and you will regret it. Trust me on that one."

"Call me more often, and have that wife of yours get on the phone once in a while and I will think about it."

"Okay Mom, I hear you."

"Tell me that you love me," ordered his mother.

"I love you Mom," responded Jack.

"Say it like you mean it," coaxed his mother.

"I love you Mom," he said in a softer voice.

Her "I love you too," was immediately followed by a click of the signal being broken and the accompanying dial tone.

Well that was fun. Thank you Benjamin.

It's very sad that your mother and aunt are so recalcitrant in their attitude towards one another.

It's crazy. One's in bad health and will probably die soon. But neither one of them is willing to make an effort. Unbelievably it is as if they have written each other off. And there's plenty of blame to go around here; neither one of them is an angel. What makes it really sad is that those two were inseparable as kids. They each think they've done all they can and washed their hands of the relationship.

They'll regret that when one of them has passed on.

I wanted to ask her if she ever really loved me, but I don't think it would have served either one of us any good purpose.

I agree. We refer to that as the Wisdom of Heaven.

For the record, I did travel to Las Vegas to comfort her when her husband died. In fact all four boys were there out of respect for Reuben and to comfort her. She sent tickets for the other boys. I paid my own way...$593.

Why would she do that?

I wanted to think that it was that was the extent of the available airline miles that she had, but I think it was just another subliminal message.

Why did you go?

Because it was the right thing to do.

That it was.

Yeah, right. Kathy said the same thing.

How would you feel if you heard that she had passed on?

I don't know. Numb maybe. No, that's not it. Apathetic I guess. It's been nearly fifty years since we have had anything close to a normal relationship.

Would you attend her funeral?

The boys and I used to joke that we would all attend it if for no other reason than to put a silver stake thru her heart like you are supposed to do with all vampires to insure that they are really dead.

That's a terrible thing to say but I get it now.

Yes it is a terrible thing to say, and half the time I feel guilty for feeling that way, but it takes two to make a relationship.

That it does. And with parent and child it should come so naturally.

Not here. What you just witnessed pretty much captures the essence of our relationship, and why at any given time one to three of the boys are NOT in the will.

Seriously?

As a heart attack. Oh, sorry. Poor choice of words on both our parts.

Let's stick with tragic.

You asked. Fortunately Grammy Lee was more than willing to be a mother to me, and there is not a day that goes by that I don't think of her. She was the essence of kindness and unqualified love. In fact, I attribute the good that is in me to her… and to Kathy. She always says that Grammy gave her something to work with, but that I am still very much a work in progress.

There is no doubt that Heaven left a hole in your heart that your parents should have filled…and didn't. For some people this becomes a fatal flaw.

Like Sociopaths, psychopaths and politicians.

Those too in extreme cases. But normal average people too. The exceptional ones — like you — yes Jack, you are exceptional — fill the hole with their own love, and move forward and don't dwell on the past, but look to the future, while living very much in the present. Just as you and Kathy have done with your children and now your grandchildren.

So our hearts are like donuts with holes in the center?

As an analogy.

That's ironic.

How so?

Mike and I and the twins used to cruise on Saturday night and stop at Dunkin Donuts for a dozen donuts that we would split. A dozen for a buck. You couldn't beat it.

Sounds like a fond memory.

Yes indeed. I haven't thought about that in years. Are donuts symbolic of anything else in Heaven?

Not that I am aware of but it's up to you to choose if that hole will be filled with pain, anger, and the eternal darkness of loss…Or if you will choose to fill it with light and love and have that hole shine out of you like a spotlight into your life, keeping the good memories alive. Imagine sharing the image of you and the guys cruising on Saturday nights while munching on donuts.

Everyone would think we were losers.

I beg your pardon.

You cruise for chicks, not donuts.

But you were doing it in the spirit of friendship and brotherhood.

Filling the hole like a jelly donut.

You know what I mean.

They were like my brothers.

Any regrets.

One of them is gone already.

Oh really.

How come you know so much about me and then there is stuff that you don't know?

It's complicated. You'll find out.

Okay…

Maybe you should make another call, and lighten your heart of another regret.

I know, light as a feather.

Light as a feather.

1725

"Love is like a friendship caught on fire. In the beginning a flame, very pretty, often hot and fierce, but still only light and flickering. As love grows older, our hearts mature and our love becomes as coals, deep-burning and unquenchable."

—Bruce Lee

The Last Supper. Hmmm. That's sort of ghoulish.

Don't think of it that way or you will ruin what could prove to be the most wonderful dinner date of your marriage.

No worries about calories tonight.

Not exactly what I meant either.

Maybe I should smoke that lone Cuban cigar that I have been saving since I made that $1.5M sale and Charlie took us to dinner, and laid his hands on some genuine Cuban cigars, before I walk the plank.

Are you intentionally being thick?

A little gallows humor my friend, that's all.

This is your opportunity to fill Kathy's heart with enough love to last an eternity. Do it right; make it special, for after tonight all she will have are her memories of the time that you spent together.

I don't know if I can do this and act as if all is right with the world.

But it is. Look, you have spent the day talking with everyone that you love, finding validation for your life's work. Tonight it goes beyond that, and is about you and your eternal companion and all that you have, and will forever, mean to one another.

It's going to be weird to make time with my wife knowing that you are around.

I won't be hanging around like one of your little brothers. This is a sacred time and I will be at a distance, but by the same token, close enough if warranted.

If warranted?

If something happens to upset the plan. Don't give it another thought. Now go in the house and love your wife.

"The King of the castle is home. What's for dinner?" he said in a light hearted voice that he was not yet feeling.

"You can keep bellowing, but I am not about to fetch your pipe and slippers. If you want to eat, come in the kitchen and keep me company," said Katharine O'Sullivan Lee.

"Well, if you put it that way, I'm in," he said as he entered the kitchen, walked up behind his wife of 34 years, and put his arms around her tiny waist.

"Careful, my hands are full of egg and breadcrumbs," began his wife.

"I'll take my chances," as he turned her around so that he could gaze into her blue eyes before softly kissing her on the lips that had melted his for the first time over forty years before.

"Well hello," she said.

"Hello yourself. Something smells good. What's for dinner?"

"Eggplant parmesan and Caesar salad."

"If I didn't already love you, I'd love you now. How did you manage a fancy dinner like this tonight?"

"Don't you remember, today was a half day of teaching and then half an institute day. I got home almost two hours ago. I've had time to ride the elliptical, take a shower, and I even snuck into your sauna for a few minutes."

"Wow. Had I known that, I would have been sure to be home to be your cabana boy or something," he said with a waggle of his thick eyebrows.

"Don't be a pig, it is so unbecoming for a man your age," she said with a smile.

"So how was school today? Did the little darlings treat you well?"

"They were little angels."

"Even Damien?"

"That's not his name."

"It should be."

Oh stop; *Damon* is a good little boy."

"Who are you kidding? He is a fifth grade version of a serial killer. The kid is evil. It would not surprise me to hear that the cops find him up in a bell tower some day with a rifle equipped with a telescopic sight."

"That is a terrible thing to say."

"Even his parents knew what to name that kid. Damien, Omen VI."

"What has you all revved up tonight?"

"Oh nothing. I've just decided not to take life so seriously, and to be even happier than I have been since leaving the wonderful practice of law."

"That's nice. Why the change?"

"Oh I don't know. Much as I hate to admit it, maturity may be setting in."

"Do tell!"

"Sad, but true," he said ruefully.

"I talked to Becky a little while ago, and she said that you had a nice conversation today," said his wife.

"I also talked to Dr. Bobby."

"So I understand."

"I also called my mother."

"Why would you do that? I mean that's nice, and all, but why subject yourself to that type of abuse? You could go to the dentist if you want an uncomfortable drilling in your head," she said, dipping more eggplant into her batter.

See Benjamin, I wasn't wrong about that root canal.

"So what did she have to say? How do *you* feel?"

"For starters, she wants to hear from you more," he said with a mischievous grin.

"Uh huh."

"Hey, you were like mother and daughter."

"Anything new with the wicked witch of the west?"

"Nope. Life is good so long as the batteries in the clicker don't run out, and QVC continues to take her credit card."

"Are you in or out of the will this week?"

"I don't know, and at this point, I really don't care."

"Sure you do. Anyone would," she said, laying down her spatula.

"So, why do you think my mother does not love me, first born and all?"

"My gosh Jack. That's the easiest question you have ever asked me."

"Well?"

"The short answer is that she is insane."

"Really?"

"If not insane, she is not right."

"She loves the other boys."

"She loves the person who does the most for her. That's why you boys have been replaced with this ridiculous notion that she has 'adopted daughters.' You have come so so far ... don't fall back and start questioning the person that you have become on your own and with some modest help from Grammy Lee and yours truly."

"Really."

"Yes, really."

"I even challenged her to call her sister!"

"You what?" she said, spraying some of her drink across the surface of the counter, and choking on the rest.

"You okay?" he asked, patting her on the back.

"I'm fine. Have you been drinking today?"

"No, but I did do something that may make you a teensy weensy mad."

"I know."

"How do you know? What do you *think* you know?"

"You went sky diving right?"

"Maybe. But maybe I was going to confess to having had a tryst with your best friend or something."

"Naw. Wouldn't happen."

"Because I am so honorable and faithful and have never given you a reason to question that you are the only woman for me?"

"No, because if you ever hit on Kim, she would tell me right after she cut your heart out and handed it to you."

"Ah. Good to know, and thanks for clearing that up. Yes, I went sky diving."

"Any particular reason you violated the prime directive?" she asked quietly.

"I needed to do something to shake the cobwebs loose. So I went out to Orange County, and after learning that they consider me a dinosaur because I allowed my jump certification to lapse, I did a tandem jump."

"Uh huh."

"It cleared my head, and allowed me to really assess and prioritize my life," he said earnestly.

"Do tell… well, I forgive you. As long as I am your #1 priority."

"You know you are."

"But you don't get to keep doing stupid stuff like that; I know that one of us is going to die someday, but I don't think we need to go looking for it," she said, her eyes growing into two slits, as she grabbed the front of his shirt with both of her greasy hands. "No more jumping out of airplanes. Clear?"

"Yes mother."

"Don't call me that," she implored. "Ever."

"Okay grandma."

"I much prefer that, since I know that you won't be comparing me to your moth-, female parent, when you use that title."

"True dat."

"Oh, I also bought you some new flat faced shorts to wear for when we go to the club."

"What's wrong with my regular shorts?"

"Nothing. But you look so much *better* in the flat fronts, and they make you look so *'sleem'* senor," she said, affecting a Spanish accent.

"Okay."

"Try them on before we go to bed tonight, because if they don't fit I want to exchange them tomorrow. They didn't have a lot of them left at Kohl's."

"Will do." I guess as long as I don't remove the tags she'll be able to return them for a credit. Waste not, want not, he thought to himself.

"So what's going on with you," she asked as she began to prepare the salad.

"I don't know. I woke up today and decided that the rest of my life was going to be better than anything in the first half."

"You're going to live to be 116?"

"You know what I mean."

"No, explain it to me."

"Seems strange to say, but I have determined that most people have no clue how to have fun. I mean from the time we become old enough to walk and talk we are way too serious. We don't find the humor in life. We don't joke around. We don't think we're funny."

"You do. Even if you aren't always," she teased.

"Honestly, we go through life oh so very seriously. Even today, Annie was turning Becky inside out by asking her some pretty heavy duty questions."

"So I heard."

"We miss out on a lot of the fun in life that way. I think we need to do something a little silly every day."

"So you went sky diving?"

"Yeah, but not exactly to be silly, but to feel really *alive!*"

"I hope that there are alternatives for future days," she said quietly.

"Absolutely there are. I used to trade jokes with Calvin the door man at the office downtown when I came in the morning. We always shared a laugh."

"I remember him. He was probably being polite."

"Maybe, but I don't think so. He was invisible to a lot of people."

"He is black Jack. Let's face it, we live in the South. To most people he *is* invisible."

"See, I never saw him as black. I just saw Calvin. I think the Army makes a difference in seeing people as 'green' rather than white, black, yellow, red."

"You are probably right."

"I know I am. America is nothing like the melting pot it is purported to be. Every major city has their Chinatowns, Little Saigons, little Mexico, you know."

"You're right."

"On the other hand, the Army really is a melting pot."

"I know. So, we should act silly and what else on a daily basis?"

"We are going to take more trips by ourselves, with our family, and with our friends. I want to see more of the world."

"We've seen a good bit of Europe, and the Caribbean."

"I know. But while we have our health, we are going to take more big trips with friends and family – to Disney World, to Paris, or even just over to the River. I want to help our grandkids create memories that they will carry with them the rest of their lives."

"Count me in," she said, getting excited.

"I'm even thinking that it would be fun to buy a place down Mexico way," he said.

"Wow. How do you propose we pay for that, Mr. Moneybags?"

"Honey, we are better off than 98% of the people our age. If we earmarked your pension or even just my military pension, we'd pay it off pretty quickly."

"We no speeky the language gringo!"

"So we learn. We go over to the junior college and take a class - together. Think about it. We could split our time and really enjoy life down there. We could have the kids come down whenever they can, and really have a lot of fun."

"You don't have to convince me!"

"Good, good," he said, reaching for the bottle to refill both of their wine glasses.

"And dinner is served," she said, as she moved to the table where two candles were also burning.

"Well that's a nice touch. I guess we don't need the television remote."

"No Sir, not tonight. So what else is on your mind?"

"Wow, this is fantastic," as he tasted his first bite of eggplant.

"Thank you kind Sir," she said, raising her glass in anticipation of clinking their glasses together.

"So I repeat, what else is on your mind?"

"I know that you are considerably younger than I, but do you have any regrets," he asked, making reference to the fact that she was nearly a full year younger and loved to point it out.

"Oh, I don't know. I don't think so. Well, well, maybe one."

"And what would that be?" he asked with curiosity.

"I guess living the life that my parents wanted me to live instead of the one I really wanted."

"What?" he asked, putting his fork down on the side of his dinner plate.

"You know that I wanted to be a swimmer, but my father did not fancy the idea that one of his daughters would be an athlete. It was so contrary to the way that he was raised to view women."

"Parasols, white gloves, and mint juleps."

"Exactly."

"Is that why you became a teacher like your mom?"

"Possibly, probably. Once I got to college and started the course work you know that I loved it. And student teaching was wonderful for me. It did so much to boost my confidence. After graduating and finding my first job, I couldn't imagine doing anything else for a living. Maybe daddy did know best…"

"So when you get right down to it, no regrets."

"Well, when I watch the Olympics. I wonder how far I could have gone as a swimmer, but that pretty much stopped years and years ago."

"Good to know. I would have supported you in your efforts you know."

"I know you would have been there for me. What about you?"

"Probably only one."

"What would that be?" she asked softly.

"For being a knucklehead."

"When were you a knucklehead?"

"About fifteen years ago."

"Oh," she said as a tinge of sadness entered her voice.

"Letting my marriage nearly break up was the dumbest thing I could ever have done."

"We don't have to do this," said Kathy.

"I learned in my practice that more people will divorce than stay together, and most of them will say that it was for the best, or, like my own mother, has been heard to say, that they 'couldn't take it anymore.' And, of course, there are some marriages that shouldn't go on and where divorce is the best for all parties involved."

"But ours did not end."

"No it didn't. Because you were smarter than I ever thought of being."

"You never left."

"No, but I thought about it."

"We had stopped communicating. Neither one of us was unfaithful. We just sort of hit a rough spot."

"For two smart people, we missed the signs."

"Yeah, but after you came up from that trial that you should never have taken on, we were able to correct most of those 'little things' that were problems."

"We tried to control one another, and that never works."

"And then we fell in love again."

"That we did," he said, reaching across the table, and kissing her hand.

"Remember that quote by Mignon McLaughlin: 'a successful marriage requires falling in love many times, always with the same person.'"

"It's safer and cheaper too."

"You are such a nerd sometimes."

"Oh yeah? How about, 'I love you without knowing how, or when, or from where. I love you simply, without problems or pride: I love you in this way because I do not know any other way of loving but this, in which there is no I or you, so intimate that your hand upon my chest is my hand, so intimate then when I fall asleep your eyes close.'"

"You remember."

"Of course. Pablo Neruda."

"I'm impressed," she said raising her glass in salute.

"Do you remember what we used to do for dates when I was in law school and we were as poor as church mice?"

"Yes. We would find quotes on love and decorate the mirror in the bathroom or paste them up on the walls in the apartment."

I found some of them today in a box out in the garage."

"You didn't."

I did. I want to share some of them with you now."

"Okay," she said in a bare whisper, with tears glistening in her blue eyes.

"Can you identify who said, 'You know you're in love when you can't fall asleep because reality is finally better than your dreams?' Time starts now."

"Easy peasy, Dr. Seuss," she said triumphantly.

"Show off."

"Okay, how about, 'if I had a flower for every time I thought of you... I could walk through my garden forever.'"

"Hmm. Hmmm. Browning maybe," she began.

"Which one, Robert or Elizabeth?" he asked.

"Neither one. It was Alfred Tennyson," she said with a big grin. "Remember me? Minor in English Lit?"

"Show off. So, let's try your luck with a movie quote. Movie and actor if you please."

"Bring it on tough guy."

"Ready? 'We need a witness to our lives. There's a billion people on the planet... I mean, what does any one life really mean? But in a marriage, you're promising to care about everything. The good things, the bad things, the terrible things, the mundane things... all of it, all of the time, every day. You're saying, 'Your life will not go unnoticed because I will notice it. Your life will not go unwitnessed because I will be your witness.'"

"Wow. You are pretty serious."

"Quit stalling. What movie?"

"How about, *Shall We Dance,*" she said triumphantly.

"Lucky guess. Who said it?"

"The wife."

"Are you sure?"

"Yes."

"Final answer?"

"Yes."

"Actor?"

"Susan Sarandon."

For 64,000 bonus points, what was her character name?" he said grinning, convinced that he had her on the ropes.

"Well, let's see. Mrs. Clark."

"What?"

"Jennifer Lopez hangs a banner at the dance studio that says 'shall we dance Mr. Clark?' so I *know* that the family name is Clark."

"That gets you half way home."

"Wait a minute. Does she even have a first name in the movie?"

"Yup!"

"Swear?"

"Cross my heart."

"The private detective calls her Mrs. Clark."

"Stalling...."

"Oh, you are going to die. I am about to give you her name."

"You're bluffing."

"Loser does the dishes," she challenged.

"Bring it on."

"Beverly Clark. Wash 'em and weep."

"How the heck did you know that?" he exclaimed.

"I watched it about a month ago," she said, starting to laugh.

"Cheater!"

"No rules baby, no rules when it comes to dishes."

"Do 'em together?"

"Impress me first," she said.

"So 'grow old with me! The best is yet to be.'"

"Robert Browning saves your butt," she said with a laugh as she started moving the dirty dishes to the sink.

"'I love you not only for what you are, but for what I am when I am with you. I love you not only for what you have made of yourself, but for what you are making of me,' read Jack from a tattered index card he pulled from his jeans pocket.

"I love the sentiment, but you got me on that one."

"None other than Roy Croft," said Jack.

"My turn. 'To get the full value of joy you must have someone to divide it with.'

You're on the clock Clyde."

"Really? That's the best you got? Maybe I should leave you with the dishes. That my dear is none other than Samuel Langhorne Clemens, also known as Mark Twain," he said smugly right before the wet soapy sponge hit him in the chest.

"He said, with the pomposity of an attorney," she snorted, wiping the soap suds from her hands.

"I was about to say that 'You are the finest, loveliest, tenderest and most beautiful person I have ever known and even that is an understatement,' but maybe I'll hold off on that," he said, as he pulled the wet shirt away from his skin.

"F. Scott Fitzgerald could not have said it better himself," she said, tossing him a clean dry towel from the drawer as she left the kitchen heading towards the den, "and P.S. 'If I know what love is, it is because of you.'"

"I love you too. And Hermann Hesse."

"Know it all. And take the garbage out."

"Done and done. I'd climb the highest mountain for you, swim the deepest stream, and walk over hot coals just to be near you."

"Yeah, yeah, yeah. Just take out the garbage; it will stink in the morning."

"I'll be right in."

"I'll count the minutes…"

That was quite beautiful…

Yeah. It was.

I am reminded that 'when we are in love, we open to all that life has to offer with passion, excitement, and acceptance.'

Well listen to you Benjamin, quoting John Lennon of all people.

You and your wife are wonderful together.

Yeah we are. Was that how it was with your wife?

Oh yes. 'Love must be as much a light, as it is a flame.' Henry David Thoreau was one of my wife's favorite writers. She was very much about light.

Was?

Is. Angelina is still very much alive.

Grieving for you?

Unfortunately yes.

Will she remarry?

No. I know she won't, because she was convinced that I was her one and only soul mate. I know that I will wait for her, as she will wait for me. We will be reunited.

I don't want Kathy to be alone. I don't want her to grieve for me. I'm supposed to be with her to take care of her, now and always.

And you will be.

Is that a promise?

To be sure. You also need to change your shirt.

1945

> "There are some people in life that make you laugh a little louder, smile a little bigger, and live just a little bit better."
>
> —Unknown.

It is amazing how time goes by so quickly.

That it does.

I am embarrassed at the fact that I lost touch with both of the twins. We even lived near one of them for several years and never thought to reach out.

It's never too late you know.

I found his contact information on LinkedIn and discovered that we both lived in Seattle the whole time that I was there when I was a corporate attorney for a few years.

Then you moved back here, and he stayed there.

Yep.

How long has it been since you spoke to one of them?
Probably twenty years plus.
That may be a relationship left for another day.
But it is a regret.
But one that will be given little weight.
Why is that? Are regrets weighted differently?
Actually they are.
So some regrets are greater than others?
Yes. As in this case where either one of the twins could also have reached out to you.

Sounds rather subjective. It just astounds me how easy it was not to stay in touch with such good friends from my childhood and youth. We tried to stay in touch at first but then simply got busy. Sometimes, I thought to pick up the phone, but then marriage, kids, and work all got in the way. Graduate school, field research, and life just got in the way. Then it was a matter of not having their number or email any more. I've always wondered what it would be like to sit down with them again for a coffee.

There will always be time for good friends to share light, love, and laughter.

Benjamin, I didn't even *know that Louis had died, much less have the opportunity of* visiting a dying friend before he died. That makes me a horrible friend.

Did the twins move away?
Well yeah.
And life goes on.

I guess I just feel so lousy because this is a pattern for me. First it was Mike, then I lost touch with the twins, and then there was my buddy Bruce.

Bruce?

Bruce and I were in ROTC together in college. He died ten years ago. He was only 47 or 48, with a wonderful wife and four great kids. He had cancer for the last 4 years of his life. We'd talked off and on over that time after re-connecting at a military reunion.

He had stayed on active duty, did his 20, retired as a lieutenant colonel, and was really enjoying life as he started a second career in the financial service business. Two months before he died, he called me and asked if I could come by to visit. I was smack dab in the middle of a huge trial – my last one as a matter of fact – and I said I'd come as soon as possible. A month later, it was clear he had days to live. I rushed to the hospital and did get to visit at his bedside before he passed, but he was a different guy from the one I'd spoken to only a month before on the phone. He was just hanging on and it was clear that he did not have long to live. We hadn't been best friends and we hadn't seen much of each other since college, but I know I'll always regret not going to visit him earlier when I'd had the chance. I saw his wife at the hospital that day, and she said that he had really wanted to meet with me to insure that his affairs were in order. As it was they found another attorney that could find the time. It is a regret that I obviously can't ever change. I'd give just about anything to have one last regular chat with him.

A strong friendship doesn't need daily conversation or being together. As long as the relationship lives in the heart, true friends never part.

Words are so easy, and too trite sometimes Benjamin.

Any other regrets that we should address to lighten your heart.

Yeah. I don't like the idea of missing out on seeing my grandchildren growing up. I had every expectation of being around to help my kids raise them, see them graduate from high school and college, and to dance with them at their weddings. Now all of that is off the table, and I don't understand why. I'm healthy, presumably the salt of the earth according to you, and yet I am getting taken out of the game.

You'll see them and be a part of their lives.

What, as a ghost scaring the bejabbers out of little Annie?

Your children and grandchildren are, and will always be, your greatest legacy.

How can I be part of them if all I am is a distant and ever receding memory? All kidding aside Benjamin, but isn't there any sort of appeals process here? I don't think it is my time to go on to the other side or whatever you call Heaven.

Be patient Jackson. All in due time. All in due time.

I don't have a whole lot of time left according to the clock!

Time moves in one direction, memories in another. Our responsibility is to establish a bridge between them for our legacy.

This isn't the time to wax philosophic or mystical Benjamin. I'm telling you that despite this wonderful gift you have purportedly brought to me today, I simply don't feel as if it is my time to leave this earth. There are still roads to be traveled, memories to be created, and a legacy built upon.

I'm sorry. Time is what we want most, but sometimes that which we use unwisely.

2010

"Practice kindness all day to everybody and you
will realize you're already in heaven now."

—Jack Kerouac

"It still looks to be a very nice evening out there. What say ye for a walk around the neighborhood," asked Jack.

"That sounds like a wonderful idea," as she reached for a pair of sneakers.

"Which way shall we go," he asked as he closed the door behind them.

"Why don't we take the long way?"

"Okay."

"I love this time of day," she said.

"Me too," he said somewhat distractedly.

"Look at the sky and the clouds. It almost looks like the entrance to Heaven."

"Do you think there is a Heaven, and if so, who goes there?"

"Wow, you certainly know how to sweet talk a girl," as she took his hand in hers.

"I think all good people go to heaven."

"Even lawyers?"

"Well, maybe the honest ones," she said with a smile.

"We balance out all the teachers who get to go there because they are angels in real life," said her husband.

"Why all this preoccupation with heaven and death?"

"Excuse me? If anything, blame your granddaughter for planting that particular seed in my head. Why do you think Annie wants to know about being able to recognize the people she knows in Heaven?"

"With kids, you never know. Especially at her age. She could have seen something on television or in a movie and it triggers a certain pattern of thought."

"How good a job do you think I did in balancing work and family aside from that period of time when I was crazed with trial work?"

"Except for those three or four years, I think you did a pretty good job. I think going on your own was a good move, but then you got too big, and had to scale back. Clearly the money was not worth it. Sacrificing the short term for the long term nearly cost us everything."

"I know."

"But it didn't Jack. And we are better than ever. The flaw in your theory of 'I'll stay late this one time and make it up with the family this weekend,' didn't work because a) the late nights became too frequent, and b) you weren't around most weekends because of the Army. You weren't trying to serve two masters, but rather three, and there was simply not enough Jack to go around. Days and weeks turned to months and then years and then we hit the wall."

"I'm sorry. I was blind and stupid."

"Jack, it is all in the past. Life is good now. I'll teach one more year, max out my pension, and then we'll really look into doing everything you were suggesting at dinner. I really like the idea of learning Spanish and getting a place down in Mexico. There is something really captivating about the whole idea of our becoming ex-pats and living life large, all the while still being attentive to our family."

"You really like the idea that much?" he said, his smile radiating across his face.

"Absolutely. For fear of swelling your head, I would say it was a stroke of genius actually. Anything else you want to change now, until we move on to the next phase of our life together?"

"Yeah. I want to make a rule that we turn off our phones more, and get off the internet. I hate it when we are with the kids and grandkids and they never get off their smart phones. It's literally an addiction."

"You're right."

"We need to set the example. I am leaving my phone in my study from now on. It will never be in the bedroom again."

"What, Mr. Realtor is not going to sleep with his phone next to him any longer? I am shocked. I am impressed, and I am so crazy stupid in love with you."

"Life is too short Kath to be tethered to these damn things. We carry it with us constantly. I leave it on the floor when I am in the shower, just in case I see a new email come in. I am tired of constantly checking email and Twitter in the evenings and on weekends just on the off chance that I might miss something. That is not living in my book."

"I agree."

"I'm only sorry that I did not think of it years ago. I get angry with myself when I think about the quality time with family and friends that it has robbed me of, and what a dope I have been."

"You know, 'for a guy with a slow leak in his head, sometimes you think real good,'" said Kathy.

"Oh, quoting Benjamin Franklin Pierce now," he said approvingly.

"I don't always agree with Hawkeye's lechery and general character, but I have to give the devil his due."

"Hey, M*A*S*H was a great show for a lot of years."

"It was, but give me one other memorable line of worth from that show, and I'll buy you an ice cream."

"I like to go swimming with bow-legged women and swim between their legs," he exclaimed almost immediately.

"Aside from the fact that Colonel Potter said that, it is not a line of *worth*, and therefore no ice cream for you."

"One more chance," he pleaded.

"I know that I am going to regret this, but go ahead," she said shaking her head.

"Ladies and gentlemen, take my advice, pull down your pants and slide on the ice," he said exultantly.

"How can such a brilliant mind and sensitive heart be housed in the same body that gives me thoughts like that," she asked.

"It's why you love me."

"It's why I love you, and am in love with you for ever and ever."

"I love you to infinity and beyond."

"Wow. That much," she said raising an eyebrow.

"And a million red M&M's."

"Now you are simply talking foolishness."

"So 'don't walk behind me; I may not lead. Don't walk in front of me; I may not follow. Just walk beside me and be my friend,'" he said dramatically.

"You're on a roll tonight mister. Albert Camus to boot."

"I'm not just another pretty face you know," he said squaring his shoulders.

"So sing something to me Casanova," she said taking hold of his arm as they walked up one of the berms that ran alongside the walking trail.

"'Ooh you're the best friend that I ever had, I've been with you such a long time.

You're my sunshine and I want you to know, That my feelings are true, I really love you, Oh you're my best friend.'"

"Wow. Queen. You *really* know how to sweep a girl off her feet."

"It's all about the sentiment."

"That it is, that it is."

"Do you ever think about what Heaven is like," he asked as he kicked a rock down the path.

"Oh I don't know. I guess we all think about it from time to time."

"What do you think it is like?"

"I *hope* that it is a place where I will be surrounded by my family and friends, and that there is peace, and no war, and no sickness, and no suffering, and that we can bask in the Glory of God."

"Wow, for someone who has not thought about it, that is one heck of a wish list," he said with a wry smile.

"I have to believe that we will be with our family and that it will be all about the love we have created here on earth."

"I sure hope you are right. Sounds wonderful," he said as they stopped to watch the sun sink a little lower in the sky.

2100

"A friend is one that knows you as you are, understands
where you have been, accepts what you have become,
and still, gently allows you to grow."
—William Shakespeare

"I'm going to take a quick bath," said Kathy as they walked back
into the house.

"I'm going to straighten out a few things on my desk, and will let
the dogs out, and meet you in the kitchen for a snack."

"It's a date."

*Jackson. I have been thinking about what you said earlier, and want
you to meet a few people.*

Is this when you bring in the big guns to convince me that I am
wrong or simply being stubborn?

Not at all. Heaven's Code does not operate along the lines you are painting.

Okay. Bring them on in.

Jackson Lee, meet Jackson Lee.

Oh, my gosh. Uncle Jackson?

In the flesh so to speak. It has been a long time since I have been able to say that and not attract some stares.

You're young. With a perfect body. No wounds.

There are no Purple Hearts awarded in Heaven, quipped his uncle.

Why are you in your WWII khaki uniform?

Because it is what differentiates me. It is how I knew you would know me. I was killed long before you were born. Your dad was only eight years old when I was killed. It's how I knew you would not only recognize me, but truly know me. In your mind, ever since Grammy Lee started talking to you about me, I have always been PFC Jackson Lee, killed at age 22, somewhere in Italy because General Mark Clark did not take us off the line. I know that she found solace in being able to blame General Clark, but he was a good man too, and did me no wrong.

That's pretty much been all I ever heard from her.

And?

Well, also how your Serviceman's Group Life Insurance policy afforded them the ability to buy the building that they lived in back in the '40s.

Anything else?

Yeah, that you were one heck of a card player, and won a lot of money off of the guys in your unit. That you used to send that home to help out the family as well.

Mom didn't tell you that.

No, actually it was my dad who shared that tidbit with me.

I could hold my own.

Sounds like you were a hustler.

Some may have felt that way after we played. But I never cheated, and always thought it was just a case of luck and my desire to do right by my family back home.

Grammy gave me the pen and pencil set with your – our – name on it that the people at the A&P gave to you before you shipped out. I display it proudly in a curio table in our family room along with all of your awards and decorations, as well as your picture.

It nearly killed both my mother and father when I didn't come home, he began somberly.

I know. I actually met a woman who knew your mom before you di— while you were alive – and she described Grammy as an extrovert, and happy go lucky type of person. I never saw that persona.

No, she suffered a broken heart. And my dad suffered even more.

So I understand.

Thank goodness your Uncle Darby came home safe from the Marines. I don't think they would have survived losing two sons. My heart still aches for the Sullivans – losing five sons all at once when the Navy ship on which they were serving went down off the Solomons.

They were aboard the cruiser *U.S.S. Juneau* during the Battle of Guadalcanal. Apparently the acting task force commander was so fearful of taking additional losses due to torpedoes that he skedaddled after the battle and did not even look for survivors.

Correct. Other survivors confirmed that Frank, Joe, and Matt died instantly, Al drowned the next day, and George survived four or five days before he succumbed. It was a tragedy of epic proportions. Five sons gone in the twinkling of an eye. I can't imagine the pain that their parents endured.

FDR wrote a letter of condolence to their parents, but what can one say in that situation?

Ah, that Franklin. He always has something to say.

They were all too young to die.

Weren't we all? I've been dead seventy two years. I was only 22 when I died. I never got to marry, have children, or to leave the type of legacy that you have created.

Are you angry about that?

There is no place for anger in Heaven. Only light, laughter, and love. I am with my parents and both of my brothers now. What is there for me to be sad or angry about when I am surrounded by those who love me? You have carried on my name in an admirable manner, and added to the Lee legacy.

I hear what you are saying, but I don't believe that it is my time to join the ranks of Heaven quite yet.

Maybe it is, maybe it isn't. But good soldiers follow orders.

And I understand that you were a good soldier. There were not many Bronze Stars awarded to PFCs in WWII.

I did my duty as I saw it. That is what being an obedient servant and soldier is all about. I have had many wonderful conversations about obedience, service, duty, and honor with our distant cousin Bobby.

Bobby?

You may know him better as General Robert E. Lee. To those of us in Heaven, he is just plain Bobby.

Oh really?

We play chess together. I usually win.

Would he agree with that statement if he were here?

I suspect he would in the end, because he is an honorable man, but he would probably attempt to make an excuse at first. Why don't you ask him yourself?

Hello Jackson, it is a pleasure to meet you.

"I must be hallucinating," said Jackson aloud.

I can assure you Sir, that you are not hallucinating and that this conversation is indeed taking place.

It is an honor to meet you Sir.

Honors that you speak of are for the earth. In Heaven we are all merely family.

It has always been an honor for me to know that we were distant relatives, as well as of Light-Horse Harry Lee.

Father? He is a good soul. Just so you know, he prefers to be called 'Governor', even though it has been a couple of hundred years since he served. His life ended rather tragically I am afraid.

I know. But what a giant of a man.

I was only a mere lad of eleven when he died.

His tribute to George Washington was incredible, and thru it, he also immortalized himself as well.

Ah yes. 'First in War, first in peace, and first in the hearts of his countrymen…second to none in the humble and endearing scenes of private life.'

My wife and I have visited the Stratford homestead.

A lovely place to have grown up.

You know that you are still revered for not taking command of the Union Army and following your heart back to the bosom of Virginia.

So I am led to believe. I merely did my duty as was required of any good solider. I think it better to do right, even if we suffer in so doing, than to incur the reproach of our consciences and posterity.

Even at Appomattox you were viewed as possessing great bearing and commanded the respect of everyone, to include General Grant.

Sam was a good man too. Loved his whiskey a bit too much. I liked my whiskey too, that is why I didn't drink it.

My wife and I have visited many of the battlefield sites in and around Virginia, and of course Gettysburg.

It is well that war is so terrible – otherwise we would grow too fond of it.

I imagine that you are here because Benjamin has enlisted your assistance in persuading me that I am in error to question whether it is in fact my time to join all of you.

Something like that to be sure and in light of the lateness of the hour, I will share only two things with you: first, in all my perplexities and distresses, the Bible has never failed to give me light and strength.

And second?

The education of a man is never completed until he dies.

But that does not say *when* he is to die.

That's true my good Colonel. But a decision such as that is well above this soldier's command authority. I now bid you adieu. And for the record, I hold my own in chess with your uncle, said Robert E. Lee, with a wink of his eye as he straightened his sash, belt buckle, and saber.

Very impressive Benjamin. Clearly you have connections.

I am only attempting to discharge my assigned duties.

Uh huh.

Perhaps someone more contemporary would be more appropriate to aiding you in your dilemma.

Sure. I've got plenty of time.

Jackson, I am going to bring someone to talk to you that may give you pause. He too died at a relatively young age, and long before people thought he should die given his stature. He had fame, fortune, and everything to live for as well. He was more fatalistic about it.

Oh, is that my shortcoming? I'm not fatalistic enough to make the team?

I believe you will recognize him.

Hello Jackson.

Steve Jobs?

Yes.

Wow. It's an honor to meet you Steve. I have long admired your work, but more importantly how you went about it.

Sometimes when you innovate, you make mistakes. It is best to admit them quickly, and get on with improving your other innovations.

Well you certainly did that, and far more. Has anyone ever anointed you the Thomas Edison of our time?

Actually no.

Well, in my mind that is what and who you were.

That is kind of you to say so. I just always believed that innovation distinguishes between a leader and a follower.

Well clearly, you were a great leader and innovator.

It's really hard to design products by focus groups. A lot of times, people don't know what they want until you show it to them. So I would design something with what I thought people had in mind and then present it to them.

I learned to do the same thing in the army while working on the general staff. The rule of thumb was never to ask a general what he thought, but rather to give him a couple of choices from which to choose. It was far less painful that way.

It is all about having a vision.

It just always astounded me how you could be so creative in things that you and your team designed. I know that most of the company's innovations came from your own imagination.

Design is not just what it looks like and feels like. Design is how it works.

But you not only figured out how it works, you made it into something special, and made things that were mere science fiction a few years ago into reality. And if it had your name on it, a consumer knew they could buy it for it would be glitch free.

I always wanted our company to be a yardstick of quality. Some people aren't used to an environment where excellence is expected.

Especially in today's disposable society. If it doesn't work, chuck it, and buy something new. Then of course there is the entire entitlement mentality – the kids today want what it took us years to achieve and they want it now. Work is an ugly word to a good number of them.

I'm convinced that about half of what separates the successful entrepreneurs from the non-successful ones is pure perseverance.

So how did you do it without ever becoming discouraged?

Sometimes life is going to hit you in the head with a brick. Don't lose faith.

That's a great attitude, but how did you live it?

Being the richest man in the cemetery didn't matter to me. Going to bed at night saying we've done something wonderful, that's what mattered to me.

I could not agree more.

I wanted to put a ding in the universe.

Well you most certainly did that. And more.

I also discovered that my favorite things in life don't cost any money. It's really clear that the most precious resource we all have is time.

That is my point. I don't think I have used up all the time that has been allotted to me. If I have, then I want affirmation of it before I willingly leave this earth.

No one wants to die. Even people who want to go to heaven don't want to die to get there. And yet death is the destination we all share. No one has ever escaped it. And that is as it should be, because Death is very likely the single best invention of Life. It is Life's change agent. It clears out the old to make way for the new.

That's a pretty powerful argument Steve.

I created a lot of cool things in my life. None of them compare with Heaven.

Don't you miss your family? Don't you feel like you were cheated out of time?

Not when the alternative is Heaven, and you still get to be there for your family.

I don't know what to say to that. It is all so…

Overwhelming.

Yes. Overwhelming. Thank you.

Jack, there's a chapter in Heaven's Code for each of us. You just need to read yours to know the truth of it all.

Well, this evening proves that Friedrich Nietzsche was clearly wrong, said Jack.

How so?

Because he said 'In heaven, all the interesting people are missing,' and clearly that is not the case if you are there.

Thank you Jack. Good luck regardless of the outcome. See you around Benjamin.

Thank you Steve. What do you think Jack?

What do you want me to say? That it was amazing to meet my uncle? To actually sate my appetite as an amateur historian by having a conversation with Robert E. Lee? To converse with a true genius in Steve Jobs? Yes, it was all those things. But I am the guy who believes in the long shot. I am the eternal optimist. When my grandson was given a 1% chance of survival, I told my son that someone has to be in that 1% and it might as well be him. So, am I convinced that it is my time now? Sorry, and don't be angry, but no.

No worries Jack. As I have told you, there is no anger in Heaven. I just don't want you to be disappointed. For as my friend Coco Chanel says, 'Don't spend time beating on a wall, hoping to transform it into a door.'

2200

"All the world's a stage, and all the men and women merely
players: they have their exits and their entrances; and one man
in his time plays many parts, his acts being seven ages."
—William Shakespeare

**"And in local news, the city unanimously enacted an ordinance
that will make it legal for medical marijuana to be available in state
controlled facilities. Previously these facilities were only accessible
in unincorporated portions of the county….Next in Weather, hear
about the warm up that is on the way…"**

The Ten O'clock news. Won't have to worry about anything after
tonight. Since I am dying 'today' I guess I have something less than two
hours now if the date on the death certificate is to be believed.

I wonder what happens if I just don't decide to die. That's stupid.
Or is it? Maybe this is like the movie *Groundhog Day* and the day does

not end until I go to sleep. What if I get on a plane and fly west? Does the day continue for me? Now you really are sounding like an idiot. No wonder Benjamin looks at you like you have two heads and both are competing to come up with the next dumb comment.

What you are experiencing is quite the norm Jackson.

Well hello Benjamin. I was wondering if you were still lurking around the neighborhood.

I don't think my duties would be or should be categorized as lurking.

Sorry, didn't mean to offend.

None taken. Offense is another one of those negative emotions that we don't engage in.

Of course not. What could I have been thinking?

No worry.

I assume that sarcasm is another negative duality that you no longer recognize since your own transition.

Recognized but not given any credence.

Ah. Thanks for clarifying that for me.

"Do you want another cup of coffee before I turn it off," is the question that rings from the kitchen.

"I don't think so."

"You seem distracted," said his wife, walking into the family room.

"No just listening to the good news that we'll be able to buy weed when we want it right here in town," he began.

"Medical marijuana," she corrected.

"Weed is weed. Medical or otherwise."

"What do you care? You have never even tried it once in your life Mister Straight Arrow. In fact, I remember when you almost beat the tar out of that friend of yours when you found out he was carrying weed in his pocket while riding in your car!"

"He could have gotten us both in big trouble. I was heading into ROTC, and he was heading off to Harvard of all places. What the heck was he thinking?"

"Maybe he wasn't thinking, and was only out for a good time?"

"He was an idiot."

"Whatever happened to him?"

"No clue."

"Oh. So why does this bug you so much?"

"I don't know. It just seems wrong to continue to legalize all these things that we know are bad for us and for the kids that don't know any better."

"People would say that it is wrong for us to drink wine," she countered.

"What? Compare weed to the fruit of the vine? What nonsense is this? I mean there was manna from Heaven, fish and loaves to feed the masses, and wine to get them schnockered."

"What are you doing? Rewriting history to suit your needs," she said with a laugh.

"No, just realizing how our society continues to go downhill, and how much more difficult it is going to be to help raise our grandchildren in this very scary world."

"Amen to that," she said, taking a seat on the sofa next to him. "What else is going thru that peanut-sized brain of yours?"

"Peanut-sized?"

"I take it back. It's not peanut sized. That's not fair to all the peanuts in the world."

"Or Mr. Peanut for that matter."

"That's true too. Actually I think you have three different squirrel cages in that head of yours and all of them have these frantic little squirrels running on these wheels at different speeds and in different directions and that is why you are the way you are," she said, biting him on the ear.

"You are a crazy woman. Your mommy and daddy did not raise you right in the head," he said pinning her arms to her side.

"You are the crazy one," she began.

"Boy, if that's not the pot calling the kettle black," he retorted.

"I like you. A lot," she said pinching his chin and kissing his lips, as she freed her arms from him.

"I'm kind of partial to you too," he said, kissing her back.

"Today was a good day," she said.

"You think?" he asked, as his heart fluttered. *I hope you'll be able to say that when the coroner tells you that time of death made today not such a great day for me.*

"Very much so."

"Why?"

"Because our kids are healthy, we have beautiful grandchildren even if they do stump us with their questions, and we have the rest of our lives to love one another."

"True dat. I was working out this very morning, and when I took stock, I came to the same conclusion that we really do have a good life together."

"Yes we do."

"In fact when I was saying my prayers this morning, and got thru saying thanks for all the bounty in our lives, I was actually trying to think of something that I would complain about, and you know what, I couldn't think of a single thing except one."

"Uh oh. What was that one thing?"

"My extended family."

"Oh. Well, yeah, you have every right to be unhappy with the way that all turned out. But it is not normal."

"I don't disagree. In fact I was reading the other day something that Fred Rogers once said."

"Fred Rogers as in Mr. Rogers Neighborhood Fred Rogers," she asked.

"Yeah. It was pretty profound."

"Do tell."

"He wrote that 'part of the problem with the word 'disabilities' is that it immediately suggests an inability to see or hear or walk or do other things that many of us take for granted. But what of people who can't feel? Or talk about their feelings? Or manage their feelings in constructive ways? What of people who aren't able to form close and strong relationships? And people who cannot find fulfillment in their lives, or those who have lost hope, who live in disappointment and bitterness and find in life no joy, no love? These, it seems to me, are the real disabilities.' I read that and immediately thought of how being truly *dysfunctional* is tantamount to being disabled. It really made me feel sad for my mom, my aunt, and their parents because my grandmother did not talk to her brother or sister for years and years."

"I've told you that it is a miracle that you are as normal as you are, and that you did not perpetuate some of these really sick — I mean — bad habits."

"But other than that one, and granted it is a doozie, I have nary a complaint," he said, slapping his hands on his thighs and nodding his head.

"No major complaints from this peanut gallery," said Kathy.

"Oh, so you do have some *minor* complaints?"

"Well, I guess it would be nice if we could figure out some place for you to put your sweaty, nasty, gnarly, workout clothes when you come home from the Y. You never used to sweat like you do now," she said with a smile. "It's darn right gross."

"Oh really? Darn right gross huh?"

"We should burn some of your t-shirts — the collars are brown. Yeuch."

I'm going to be dead in less than two hours, and she is going to have to remember that one of the last things we talked about is how nasty my workout clothes become now. Quick, change the subject. Say something patently stupid that only you can say.

"Well there is a solution."

Well, don't hold out on me. Spill it," she said, encouraging him by waving her hands in a 'come on' manner.

"Mind you this is just a rough idea that just came to me," he said as a buildup, "but we *could* hire a young little Chiquita named Maria *now* to bee bop around here wearing a short little maid's uniform while *she* takes care of the *casa*, cooks some *arroz con pollo* or *carne asada* and other vittles, all the while she takes care of my nasty, gnarly workout clothes, help us with our Spanish lessons, and laughs at all of my wonderfully entertaining and witty jokes."

"You remember what I said earlier about you thinking real good despite the slow leak in your head," asked his wife.

"Si, senora."

"Forget it. You don't think real good."

"So no little Chiquita?"

"Uh no. We could not find anyone who would be willing to handle those nasty clothes for what we would be willing to pay her. Of course if we bought her a flame thrower, and you left your clothes in the backyard in the fire pit, maybe it would work. And, unless she spoke no English, she would eventually tire of your worn out jokes just as your own children, your brothers, and your beautiful wife have all also done so after years of repetition. So, no Maria."

"How about a *Brigitte*, and a little *oh la la* around the house?"

"Nope. Never been much of a Francophile except when we are visiting their country and enjoying escargot and a good Bordeaux. Don't want any little French girls running around the house to distract you from *your* chores."

"Every party needs a pooper, that's why we invited you. Party pooper," he said, affecting a Germanic accent.

"You're crazy, do you know that?" she asked stifling a laugh.

"Only about you. So will you be my little Chiquita and allow me to chase you around our new *casa* and to make mad passionate love to you while the waves crash on the beach outside our window?"

"I will allow you to chase me around our new little *casa* and *may* even allow you to catch me from time to time old man," she said as she plopped down on his lap.

"Who are you calling old, old lady?" he asked menacingly.

"Seriously, do you really still want to chase me around the house, or would you prefer a young pert Maria or Brigitte?"

"I only have eyes for you," he began.

"Oh, I love that song. Art Garfunkel."

"Yes, but he didn't do it first."

"No? Yes he did."

"Oh no, no, no. That song has been around since 1934."

"What?"

"Oh yeah."

"Nuh uh. You're making that up."

"Written by Harry Warren and Al Dubin for the film *Dames* where it was introduced by Dick Powell and Ruby Keeler. It was a #2 hit for Ben Selvin that same year."

"How do you keep all that useless trivia from leaking out of your ears," she said marveling at his recall of facts and dates.

"Do you want to know all the other movies that it has appeared in," he asked, feigning innocence.

"No. No. I surrender. You are still the undisputed king of the trivia board."

"See, that didn't hurt did it?"

"You are such an idiot some times."

But loving you with every fiber of my being at this moment, creating a memory that you can hold on to for ever and ever.

"My love must be a kind of blind love, I can't see anyone but you," he began to sing softly.

"Are the stars out tonight, I don't know if it's cloudy or bright," she responded.

"I only have eyes for you," they sang in unison.

"The moon may be high, but I can't see a thing in the sky," he whispered into her ear, and gently kissed her. "I only have eyes for you."

"I don't know if we're in a garden, or on a crowded avenue," she sang in response.

"You are here, and so am I," he sang, his voice catching.

"Maybe millions of people go by," she sang as a tear rolled down a cheek.

"But they all disappear from view," he continued with effort to control his emotions.

"And I only have eyes for you," they sang in unison as they embraced.

"First one in bed gets the remote," he said, attempting to lighten the mood with every fiber of his being.

"Let the dogs out again, and I'll share the remote, after you chase me around the *casa*," she said with love in her eyes.

"Brazen hussy," he said, as he watched her run out of the room.

"Si senor."

"Come on Max, come on Bo, outside," he called to the dogs ensconced on the recliner and sofa, as he also began turning out the lights for the last time.

2320

"The connections we make in the course of a
life—maybe that's what heaven is."

—Fred Rogers

The flames from the fireplace in their bedroom were casting flickering shadows on her face as he stared down at her sleeping form attempting to frame in words all of the emotions that were running through his heart, mind, and soul.

Kathy, I love you. You have been the light in my life. When I say it's that special element or sparkle that makes you the person I like, I'm talking about that part of you that has made me into so much better a person. Without being cliché, you made me want to be a better man. Who said that hmmm? Yeah, it was Jack Nicholson in *As Good As It Gets*. I love that part of your heart that has connected with mine, and taught me to experience the world with all of my senses. For you have taught me that life has more color, is more vivid and bold, when we experience it with our heart as well as our regular senses. You nearly gave me the same gift that Annie Sullivan gave to Helen Keller, allowing her to see and hear and touch when her senses had failed her. Wait, that sounds a little over the top. I mean that would make you a miracle worker and we wouldn't want to swell your head. I know, I'm an idiot. But I am an idiot so in love with you, and so grateful that you decided that you wanted to fall in love with me too.

I don't understand why it is my time to leave you now, but sometime in the next thirty six minutes, that is what is going to happen. Since the likelihood of my getting hit by a train or a bolt of lightning are pretty slim lying in bed next to you, I guess there is another masterful exit planned for me.

I hope that the time we spent together tonight did in fact fill your heart with even a tenth of the love that I feel in mine at this moment. We may not get our chance to have a *casa* down Mexico way, but I will be waiting for you with a big wet kiss when it is your time to come through the veil after which we will be together for eternity. Look for me, I'll be the good looking guy in a tuxedo saving you a seat with a chilled bottle of Bordeaux and a single red rose. Be forewarned that I may just be wearing one of my gnarly workout t-shirts under the tux shirt because in heaven we don't perspire, and so I won't be gross. Richard Gere has nothing on me baby!

I *really* don't know why we are not going to get to be allowed the time we had planned to spend together here on earth in our golden years. It seems like only yesterday that you were getting your braces off of your teeth, went to prom with someone else, went away to another school to assert your independence, but agreed to go out when we were both home over Christmas break. I knew that you would fall in love with me if we reconnected because you never ever left my heart. Who's the idiot now baby!

You took pity on me and accepted my incredibly romantic proposal of marriage and we went to law school and had our babies. If I ever doubted the existence of a God, those doubts were immediately dispelled the minute I laid eyes on our babies. I mean the odds of even having a normal healthy baby are astronomical if one considers that with the slightest of permutations of just one DNA strand, and you can end up with something that has a tail. Hmm. Becky with a tail. She would still be cute. I know, I'm an idiot. Don't mention the tail to Becky. Now Bobby with a tail would be kind of funny. Maybe like Jason Alexander in *Shallow Hal.* I must be getting light headed as I start to head through the stratosphere. Why else would such stupid stuff be coming out of my mouth? You're right; it's because I don't want this moment to end. I don't want to be separated from you. Because I don't place a whole lot of stock in being able to communicate with you like a dead Patrick Swayze does with Demi Moore in *Ghost. Ughh.* I hate it when those goblins come and take the bad guys away. But again, I digress.

I'm glad that you were never one of my elementary school teachers. I would have failed miserably because I would have sat there fantasizing about you, and what it would be like to hold your hand or to kiss your lips. It would still be G-rated at that age. As it was I had a pretty hot fifth grade teacher who wore short mini-skirts, but next to you, she's a pit bull in drag. Of course, having to repeat a year with you as my teacher would have had its advantages.

I don't know if you will receive any of these thoughts from me, but I would like to think that with our hearts being as close as they were, and the fact that after all the years we spent together that we could finish one another's sentences that you will know how much I love you.

While I don't want you to grieve and live a lonely life, I've got to tell you that the idea of another guy sitting in my recliner, helping you spend the insurance money, and carving the turkey at Thanksgiving is not setting well with me. Maybe after I am angelic figure it will feel different, but you always said that if something happened to you first, leaving me behind, that I was <u>NOT</u> allowed to remarry, so I guess what is good for the gander is good for the goose as well. So, live your life, enjoy our kids and grandkids, and even great grandkids, but remember that I'll always be close by, and definitely waiting for you, so no men for you!

Well, enough rambling I guess. I may even see my ride coming. I used to hate it when I had to travel for work or the army, but at least I always knew that you would be there when I got home. I don't know what home is going to be like until we are together again, but I know that my heart won't be complete without you there leaving all the lights on just like your dad warned me. 'Honus' he said, 'you will spend the rest of your life turning lights out after my baby girl, and while I can't promise you that she'll ever stop turning them on with any intention of turning them off, I will tell you that it will be worth your while.' He was right, it's been more than worth it.

I love you, to infinity and beyond, more than a *trillion, billion zillion* red M&Ms, and with all my heart.

2345

"We may speak about a place where there are no tears,
no death, no fear, no night; but those are just the benefits
of heaven. The beauty of heaven is seeing God."
—Max Lucado

Are you ready Jack?
Do I have to be?
Well, it helps.
Do I have a choice?
We always have a choice.
Benjamin, what if I don't want to go because I don't think I have
finished what I need to do here? Is there someone I can speak to about
staying longer?
*Jack, the beauty of Heaven is eternal glory. It is not a game show where
one makes a deal that thwarts Heaven's Code.*

I just always figured that when my time really came, that I would want to go because I knew that it was the right time to go. That it would be along the lines of how Erma Bombeck expressed it.

Erma Bombeck? Explain.

I remember it verbatim. She wrote, "When I stand before God at the end of my life, I would hope that I would not have a single bit of talent left, and could say, 'I used everything you gave me.'"

A noble sentiment indeed.

I don't think that I am quite there yet.

Nobody ever thinks that their time has truly come.

Oh, I would respectfully disagree. I have known many older people who have known it was their time, and quite literally told their family that it was time, laid down, went to sleep, and never woke up. My wife's grandmother did it!

Hmm. This does not usually happen.

Sorry, but I am taking Bobby Lee at his word and looking to the Bible.

Ecclesiastes 3:1-11,

[1] **To everything there is a season, and a time to every purpose under the heaven:**

[2] A time to be born, and a time to die; a time to plant, and a time to pluck up that which is planted;

[3] A time to kill, and a time to heal; a time to break down, and a time to build up;

[4] A time to weep, and a time to laugh; a time to mourn, and a time to dance;

[5] A time to cast away stones, and a time to gather stones together; a time to embrace, and a time to refrain from embracing;

[6] A time to get, and a time to lose; a time to keep, and a time to cast away;

[7] A time to rend, and a time to sew; a time to keep silence, and a time to speak;

⁸ A time to love, and a time to hate; a time of war, and a time of peace.

⁹ What profit hath he that worketh in that wherein he laboureth?

¹⁰ I have seen the travail, which God hath given to the sons of men to be exercised in it.

·¹¹ He hath made every thing beautiful in his time: also he hath set the world in their heart, so that no man can find out the work that God maketh from the beginning to the end.

This is highly irregular.

Again, I am sorry. But I can no sooner ignore these words than I can my feelings.

Gather your thoughts. Time is nigh.

2355. Nothing like cutting it close. Well, I am not going to die in bed. I swore that I never would. That is too creepy, and I am not going to do that to Kathy. I am getting up. Teddy Roosevelt would not go down without a fight, nor will I.

Teddy, you may not be listening, but you have long since been a hero to me. Like you, I had asthma as a kid, and I too outgrew it. Your life story was an inspiration to me, and I look at your 'Man in the Arena' quite often. In fact, it is hanging on the wall in the hall outside my study; I must see it again before I see you.

"It is not the critic who counts; not the man who points out how the strong man stumbles, or where the doer of deeds could have done them better. The credit belongs to the man who is actually in the arena, whose face is marred by dust and sweat and blood; who strives valiantly; who errs, who comes short again and again, because there is no effort without error and shortcoming; but who does actually strive to do the deeds; who knows great enthusiasms, the great devotions; who spends himself in a worthy cause; who at the best knows in the end the triumph of high achievement, and who at the worst, if he fails, at least fails while daring greatly, so that his place shall never be with those cold and timid souls who neither know victory nor defeat."

His eyes then wandered to the grandfather clock in the dining room. The pendulum slowly and quietly clicking back and forth. 2357,

2358, 2359. And at midnight it began its Westminster chiming, four sets of four chimes, followed by twelve gongs.

He involuntarily closed his eyes, and there was darkness, the slowly fading reverberation of the clock's chimes, the only noise in the house, followed by a very bright light.

Morning

"Write it on your heart
that every day is the best day in the year.
He is rich who owns the day, and no one owns the day
who allows it to be invaded with fret and anxiety.

Finish every day and be done with it.
You have done what you could.
Some blunders and absurdities, no doubt crept in.
Forget them as soon as you can, tomorrow is a new day;
begin it well and serenely, with too high a spirit
to be cumbered with your old nonsense.

This new day is too dear,
with its hopes and invitations,
to waste a moment on the yesterdays."

—Ralph Waldo Emerson

The Morning After in the bright light of the SICU.

"Jack. Jack. Jackie. Wake up Jack. The procedure was a complete success. You passed out when you got up to go to the bathroom in the middle of the night and you suffered a mild heart attack. Don't you remember it?" asked Dr. Stanley Waters.

"Where am I?" asked Jack groggily.

"Jack, you are going to be completely fine. You are in the SICU – the surgical intensive care unit at St. Mary's. Do you remember anything since you went to bed last night?" asked his doctor.

"No. Wait. I went to bed with Kathy, and got up so that I wouldn't, uh, uh, I don't remember," he began as he realized that he was still alive and had the impression that he should not share his experience of the past twenty four hours.

"Thank goodness Kathy noticed you were not in bed and went to check for you," said Waters.

"You gave us all a scare Pop," said Robert, relief spreading across his face.

"Bobby, you're here too."

"Where else would I be dad? I had to be here," said his son, with tears in his eyes.

"You're a good boy, I mean man," said Jack. "We'll toss the ball around later."

"I think that is the funny gas talking," said the nurse.

"Oh Daddy. We didn't even know that you had a heart condition," cried his daughter as she buried her face in his neck.

"I love you too pumpkin," he said as he patted her back. "I don't have a heart condition, do I Stan?" asked Jack.

"You still have that irregular valve sequence that you have always had, but the problem that caused the heart attack has been repaired. Tricky procedure but you were in good hands."

"You didn't do it?"

"Me? I'm a GP. You may as well have asked your car mechanic to operate on you as soon as having me do it. I was in the OR to observe, and you have a brilliant surgical resident to thank for still being part of this world."

"I want to meet him."

"We can arrange that, later, when you are completely awake. Doris, page Dr. Lehrer and advise him that Mr. Lee is awake and would like to meet him at his convenience."

"Yes doctor."

"How long will I be here? I hate hospitals," said Jack.

"He hates hospitals except when babies are being born," said Kathy as she stroked his cheek, smiling down at him.

"If all goes according to plan, come tomorrow morning and I am kicking you out of here. We need these beds for legitimately sick people. A stint and an occlusion does not a sick person make," said Stan. "Now, you all can probably use some breakfast and coffee, so go down to the cafeteria and take a load off, while we allow pretty boy here to get some rest before we move him out of SICU into a regular room on the cardio floor."

* * *

"Jack, you awake," asked Stan Waters from the doorway of the room.

"Yeah," said Jack, his voice a little hoarse still from the intubation tube.

"I have someone here that you probably owe at least a good case of scotch to for saving your sorry butt," said Stan.

"Doctor, I hope you won't be tainted by Doctor Waters' inimitable bedside manner," said Jack, as he offered up his right hand.

"Frankly, I find Doctor Waters bedside manner quite fascinating, and it is apparently very reassuring to his patients," said the surgical resident.

"Jackson Lee, meet Doctor Benjamin Lehrer, Jr., MD, third year surgical resident, and all around good guy," beamed Stan Waters.

"It is a pleasure to meet you awake now Mr. Lee," said Lehrer.

"Why do I have the feeling that we have met before Doctor," asked Jack.

"Well, we did, in the OR. Of course you were still pretty much unconscious."

"No, I mean like you *look* very familiar to me, and your mannerisms are as well," said Jack.

"I'm not certain how to respond to that, Mr. Lee. Many people who know me say that I remind them of my father, but I am quite certain that you never met him," said Lehrer very methodically as if processing the information.

"Do you have family in the area doctor," asked Jack.

"No sir. I am a transplant from the greater Philadelphia area."

"Is your family still there," asked Jack.

"Yes sir. My mother still lives in the same house and my two sisters also live in the same neighborhood in which we all grew up."

"And your father?"

"He passed away about three and a half years ago," said Lehrer quietly.

"Oh, my condolences. He must have been very proud of you," said Jack with a smile.

"I know that he was, and I feel as if he never truly left us. Every so often I get the feeling as if he is looking over my shoulder, or patting me on the shoulder as he often did when he was pleased with something I had done or said," shared Lehrer.

"Well, I wish I could tell him what an apparently bang-up job you did on me this morning."

"That would make his day," said Lehrer with a smile. "He always loved hearing about any achievement of one of his children."

"What do your sisters do for a living?"

"My older sister is an OR nurse, and my younger sister is a general practice dentist. My father would say, 'I can't wait to say 'my daughter the dentist' and then sit in her chair and let her fix my teeth...for a discount.' If he said that once, he said it a hundred times. It was the only time that he was not serious," recalled Lehrer.

"What did your father do for a living? Was he in the medical field as well?"

"Oh no. He was a teacher, as his father had been before him. He taught science, and had dreamed of being a doctor himself," said Lehrer with a shrug of his shoulders.

"That's ironic since your surname is German for the word teacher. Lehrer."

"Yes, I am aware of that. It was something that my father was very proud of and wore like a badge of honor."

"He sounds like a wonderful man."

"He was a wonderful man. My only regret is that I was not able to care for him when he was taken from us."

"Oh, that must have been very difficult for you."

"Especially since I have performed the procedure that would have saved his life at least 125 times in the past three years."

"What procedure is that?" asked Jack.

"He died of an aortic aneurism that ruptured. Undetected, it was like a time bomb waiting to go off in his chest."

"Oh my gosh! How awful."

"The solace we take is that he died almost instantaneously in his classroom at school surrounded by all the books that he loved so much. He had an incredible library that he would very graciously share with his students so as to inspire, and then feed, their dreams," recalled Lehrer.

"He sounds like a wonderful man."

"Over two thousand people attended his funeral," said Lehrer proudly.

"What an incredible tribute and outpouring of love."

"He taught for more than thirty years, and inspired many of his students to achieve many marvelous things with their own lives. In several instances he taught two generations of the same family, and in a very small number, three generations."

"What an incredible legacy. You in turn must be very proud of him as he apparently was of you and your sisters."

"To him, an education was everything. Knowledge was power, and the opportunity to empower the good in people."

"It sounds like they could have created the movie *Mr. Holland's Opus* about him, and the legacy he left," said Jack.

"Very much so. Like Mr. Holland, my father often minimized the significance of his contributions even though they were obvious as more and more of his students went on to achieve great things academically and professionally," recalled Lehrer.

"What a legacy."

"I am proud to carry his name."

Benjamin. Lehrer. Teacher. You really are thick sometimes Jack, said his conscience. No, Kathy is right, I <u>am</u> an idiot.

"And your mother's name is Angelina," blurted Jack.

"Why Yes! How would you know that," asked Benjamin Jr.

"I think I may have met your father in my travels," said Jack very slowly, now wondering whether yesterday had really occurred or whether it had been a very detailed hallucination brought on by the surgery and accompanying anesthesia, or whether he was losing his mind.

"That's incredible Jack," exclaimed Stan.

"I don't know for sure. But I feel as if I know you Benjamin, if I may now call you that," said Jack.

"Please do. For no certain reason that I can fully ascertain, I feel as if I know you too, *Jackson*," he said, laboring with the name.

"Well I have legitimately sick people that I need to go and see," said Stan Waters as he buttoned his long white coat and adjusted the stethoscope around his neck. "Especially if you guys are going to do Kumbaya as an encore. Damndest thing how you pulled his mother's name out of the air like that!"

"Thank you Benjamin."

"You're welcome Jackson."

Thank you Benjamin.

Afternoon

"Good friends, good books, and a sleepy
conscience: this is the ideal life."

—Mark Twain

I've noticed several common threads in the conversations that we have had, and particularly the books you have talked about as well as those that I have seen sitting on your bookshelves. You can tell a lot about a person from the books on their shelves.

If they really read them, and were not placed there by a zealous interior decorator, quipped Jack.

That's very true. But "a room without books is like a body without a soul."

Cicero?

Quite right Jack. Good for you. It really is about books.

Thomas Jefferson thought so; he wrote "I cannot live without books."

163

Quite right. I have found that the books you really love are usually bound together by a secret thread. You know very well what the common quality is that makes you love them, though you may or may not be able to articulate why. In my mind these books tell us a great deal about who you are, what you stand for, and what you hope to be as life continues to unfold.

Now you sound like a philosopher.

No, just a humble teacher.

Don't you mean escort?

Sometimes an escort, but always a teacher. That's what you are now Jack. A teacher. You teach your children, your grandchildren, and those you labor with on a daily basis.

Your son is incredible.

He truly is. I watch him work sometimes.

He knows that you are there.

No he doesn't. He can't. It's not logical.

Yes, Benjamin he does. He says that he nearly feels your pat of approval on his shoulder after he completes a procedure. It means a great deal to him, and I think he finds both comfort and joy in it.

I cannot think of a greater joy that I have felt in a very long time than in hearing that.

There is no doubt that he is your son either. Talk about a clone. My goodness, it was like waking up to a younger version of you standing over me.

Fortunately the girls favor their mother.

Books and banal pleasantries. Do you really want to maintain this charade of small talk, or can we talk about why I am still here?

We actually are talking about why you are still here. It is because of the changes you have made in your life of late; because you are desirous of being a teacher; and of being a light in this Life.

But why was yesterday necessary? Was it a gift as you purported it was, or was it an audition? I am confused.

First, it was both Jack.

And if you only recently died, how were you there when I had a prompting to go and see Mike on the day that he died? You said 'I was there.'

Second, when I came here to escort you it was my understanding that your transition time was here, and that you were to accompany me. When this assignment was made, I was given your case file, and our lives became entwined. I <u>became</u> every spirit that had ever prompted you at any time in your earthly life.

Whoa. That is going to take some time for me to process, said Jack.

Understandable.

Then what happened?

Apparently the time was not right, or your 'appeal' was heard and favorably ruled upon. Or a lesson needed to be learned, or a reward was earned, or there is still work to be completed.

That's a lot of or's.

Jack, again, do the gates of heaven swing in or swing out?

Message received Benjamin. The reason I am still here does not matter; what is important is that I *am* still here.

Exactly. I don't know why Kathy thinks you are an idiot. You are actually quite bright, he said with a chuckle.

Benjamin, did you just make a joke?

Quite. But remember Jack, we operate on the Lord's timetable, not our own.

Thank you Benjamin.

No, thank you Jackson. It was a wonderful gift that you gave to me just now in allowing me to know that my son wears my name proudly, and that he knows that I am very pleased with him as well. There have been so many times that I wished I could reach out and touch his face, or that of my wife, or my daughters, simply to let them know that I am still nearby and watching over them.

Will I continue to see you Benjamin?

Not for a good many more years. Our time together is at the end for now, but I would hope that we will be friends in the time to come.

Oh you can count on that! But one more question if I may…

No, Jackson.

No, I can't ask you one more question?

No. The answer to your question is no.

You haven't heard my question.

I have, and the answer to your question as to whether you should tell anyone about your day yesterday is no. What is important is that you always remember it as a special gift that you opened with family and friends, and will cherish for the rest of your days.

Okay, now you are just showing off, said Jack.

It's a gift.

Wow, two jokes in the same day. Good bye Benjamin. Thank you.

Good bye Jackson, and thank you. Remember, Heaven is all about light, laughter, and love. Be a piece of Heaven here on earth.

Home

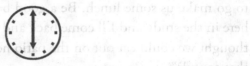

"Yesterday is history, tomorrow is a mystery, today is a gift of God,
Which is why we call it the present."

—Bil Keane

"Okay Jack, the doctor said that you need to take it easy for a few days and to be a good boy," said Kathy.

"I've always had this fantasy about you in a nurse's uniform," he said as he allowed her to help him into the large leather chair in the corner of his study.

"That will be enough of that," she said, slapping his hand playfully as he reached out to grab her bottom.

"Just wanted you to know that it was me," he said, as she bent over to gently kiss him on the forehead.

"Don't ever do that to me again Jack," she said as tears immediately came to her eyes. "I thought I had lost you."

"I'm sorry. I can't imagine what that was like for you, though I do sometimes imagine what life would be like without you, and then I have to stop thinking about it because it hurts too much."

"Exactly. MY heart almost stopped when I saw you laying on the floor in the foyer," she recalled with a shudder. "I mean I am used to you getting up at odd hours to write or read, or do whatever you do when us normal people are sleeping, but when I felt the bed empty on your side, I knew something was not right."

"Thank goodness you went with your instincts. I suppose in some small way I may just *officially* owe you my life now. I mean you have always been my life, but now I actually owe you for saving me."

"You were gray Jack," she said, plopping down on the arm of the chair, as the events of the last two days caught up with her. "I am going to go make us some lunch. Be a good boy, and don't be an idiot. Stay here in the study and I'll come back and get you when lunch is ready. I thought we could eat out on the patio next to the waterfall. How does that sound?"

"Like a little piece of heaven here on earth," he said, sitting back in his chair.

Kathy had no sooner left the room when he noticed a piece of parchment inside the book that he had been reading the night before his last day.

> *One more thing Jack… as you may have already surmised, the real gift is that you will now get to experience Another Last Day… but this time, you won't know when. So live each and every day to the fullest. Shower those around you with all the love that you are capable of mustering, remember that more than ever before, you are a heavenly being having a mortal experience, and not like the rest of the world who are largely mortals hoping to experience a heavenly experience some day. Your friend, B.*

Quietly and reverently he folded the parchment and placed it in his large book of memorabilia.

"Miss me?" she asked as she came back into the study.

"You are like oxygen to me," he replied.

"Are you hungry?"

"I could eat a horse."

"Well its salad for lunch today; we can have equine burgers over the weekend if you still have a hankering for horse by then," she said with a gleam in her eye.

"You know what the best part about today is my little Chiquita," he began, affecting a Spanish accent.

"No what? Being here with me?"

"Besides that of course."

"Okay I'll bite. What is the best part of today," she said, standing there with her arms folded across her chest, now in full anticipation for something either extremely memorable or incredibly stupid.

"Just three days ago, I plunked down fifty bucks for a five year watch battery replacement warranty. Now I know that they are going to lose money on me because I am going to make sure to take it in every year for servicing and new batteries."

"Uh huh. Anything else?"

"Yeah. I'll get to wear those shorts you bought me too. Let's take the tags off, and I'll slip into them before we head outside. The man definitely makes the clothes, and I am feeling pretty lucky just about now."

"My father was right, you are an idiot."

"Yes, but I am *your* idiot, soon to be your idiot in two languages and in two countries."

"Yes, you are. Let's go take the tags off those shorts."

* * *

"If you are sure that you are okay, I am going to run to the store for some of the stuff that they said you should be eating the next few days.

I can call one of the kids to come over and sit with you if you wish," she said, keys in hand, as they walked out of the kitchen together.

"Both Benjamin and Stan said that I am perfectly fine. I neither want nor need a babysitter. Though if you would like to do an imitation of Florence Nightingale, I suspect that a sponge bath later might be in order."

"You're impossible," she said, turning around and grabbing his chin and kissing him.

"Impossible to forget...just like you," he said, grabbing her wrist and giving her hand another squeeze. "I love you."

"I love you too. Don't do anything stupid while I am gone, and keep your phone within reach at all times in case you need me or anyone else."

"What's that number for 9-1-1- again," he asked, picking up a pencil and pad.

"Idiota."

"What?"

You heard me. Idiota. It's a term of endearment that means the same in Spanish and Italian. Figure it out."

"Adios."

Returns to his study.

On his desk are all of the materials that he had so painstakingly gathered the day before, which he will now be able to return to their rightful place in the safe reserved for important papers.

It was then that he spied a note from Kathy...

Jack:

You are the light in my life too. But a trillion billion zillion M&Ms don't buy what they used to – so make it opals and I'll stay with you forever, bad jokes and all.

P.S. You do look great in a tuxedo, and are very much worth it too, even if you are an idiot sometimes. ☺

Your caliente Chiquita, Kathy

Author's Observations

"Pay no attention to the man behind the curtain…"

-The Wizard of Oz

This is the tenth book that I have now completed. With several others in various stages of progress, the premise for this book was conceived in the shower on a Sunday morning as I prepared to go to an early morning meeting at church. I have been asked what sparked it to life. My answer is simply a heart palpitation, and the thought that many of us share from time to time: what if today is the day that I am to die?

I attended all of my meetings at church, during which my brain continued to frame up the outline of the story. I did not write anything down, and just kept hoping that I would remember all the salient points long enough to capture them on paper. Immediately after lunch I sat down to literally brain dump the entire outline of the book in about

90 minutes. While I did work my regular job every day, I was nearly possessed with the need to capture this story on paper. I would arise even earlier than normal, spent some extended lunch hours, and often wrote until after midnight. The book almost literally and figuratively "wrote itself" as the story poured out easier than anything else I have ever written. At times the emotions and memories that were being resurrected were overpowering; other times they were cathartic, while still others simply filled me with joy because they all served as a means by which to convey to all of my family just how special they are to me. It is only for this reason that I can fathom why the outlining and first draft of this book was completed in less than eleven days of part-time writing.

I hope the story also conveys the sense of peace that I have in terms of my gospel knowledge and what I sincerely believe awaits us in the next life. I've always envisioned what it would be like to talk to the uncle whom I am named after, or to historical figures such as Robert E. Lee, and contemporaries like Steve Jobs. The words they utter are largely their own molded to my needs.

The value statement that Jackson previously wrote in a leadership workshop is mine with a few revisions.

As the final revisions ae being made to the manuscript, I have had more time to spend with the story and realize that it was the book that I needed to write to capture all of my hopes and dreams for this life and the next. I do believe that Heaven is all about Light, Laughter, and Love. It has taken me more than a few years, but I am finally grasping the concept of Charity Never Faileth, and what it means to live a Christ-like life focused on family and service. I also believe that we will be judged not on the wealth and material abundance that we accumulate, but rather on what we do with our life here on earth. Like Jackson, I am contemplating what I want the final two acts of my life to be, and hope to find clarity for myself in these pages as I continue to ponder them.

While the names have been changed to protect the innocent, I hope everyone will be gracious and make allowances for the literary licenses that have been taken from time to time for purposes of the story.

We do have our "1% miracle" grandson; the 2 year old granddaughter who does ask the insightful questions; the 8 year old going on 14; as well as fourteen other grandkids of various shapes and sizes. The five children have been consolidated into only two, and the trillion, billion, zillion red M&Ms don't even come close to expressing what is in my heart. And sometimes…I am still an *idiota*.

Don Levin
Nampa, Idaho
July 2016

P.S. The conversations that I had with my brothers actually occurred almost verbatim two months *after* I completed the original manuscript when we all gathered in Texas for my brother's 50th birthday celebration. It was, as Yogi Berra was heard to say, "like déjà vu all over again."

DJL
October 2016

Other Available Titles

The Code

Knight's Code

Broken Code

The Gazebo (with Alexander Lebenstein)

Eight Points of the Compass

Don't Feed the Bears

Wisdom of the Diamond (with Tom Bartosic)

The Leader Coach (with Terry Edwards)

The Right Combination (with Todd Bothwell)

About the Author

Don Levin is the Managing General Agent of PNW Insurance Services, a national insurance brokerage, and has been in the insurance industry since 1999. Don is also a former practicing Attorney-at-Law, court-appointed Arbitrator, as well as a retired U.S. Army officer.

Don earned his Juris Doctor from The John Marshall Law School, his MPA, from the University of Oklahoma, and his BA from the University of Illinois-Chicago. He is also a graduate of the U.S. Army Command & General Staff College and the Defense Strategy Course, U.S. Army War College.

In his spare time, Don is an author, and has published nine other books in a wide range of genre. Don is very active with his church and within the community, and remains focused on his wife Susie, their five children, seventeen grandchildren and two dogs aptly named Barnes & Noble.

Don may be reached at HYPERLINK "mailto:dlevin@pnwis.com" dlevin@pnwis.com.

About the Author

Printed in the United States
By Bookmasters